The
Shaver Mystery Magazine
Vol 2 No 2 1948

Richard S. Shaver
Alfred Steber (Editor)

SAUCERIAN PUBLISHER
Original Sources in Ufology

ISBN: 978-1-955087-53-7

9 781955 087537

2023, Saucerian Publisher

PROLOGUE

Returning to the classics in any genre is generally a good idea. This also goes for UFO literature. Rereading a book or reviewing old documents after ten or twenty years is a rewarding experience. You will discover new data and ideas you didn't notice before. The reason, of course, is that you are, in many ways, not the same person reading the book the second or third time. Hopefully, you have advanced in knowledge, experience, and intellectual and spiritual discernment. A good starting point is to reread the UFO classics to understand the more profound mystery of what happened during that era.

This title is scarce and hard to find these days. The Shaver Mystery Magazine originally was published by the Shaver Mystery Club. This newsletter published the first printed stories on UFOs and was a major forum for debates about the occult, Forteans, and Lemurians. As Ray Palmer promoted it: "dedicated to the further study of the hidden truths as presented in the fact-fiction stories by Richard S. Shaver..."

In essence, the Shaver Mystery is a collection of stories in which Shaver claimed to have discovered proof of an evil humanity in underground caverns. Shaver portrayed an alien race that resided in Earth's caverns before escaping, leaving behind two distinct populations of offspring: the "Teros," a benevolent group of humanoids, and the "Deros," or "detrimental robots," a vile race who tormented and devoured humans. The Deros were especially brutal to women. The tales encouraged the establishment of Shaver Mystery Clubs.

The present edition is an authentic reproduction of the original Shaver Mystery Magazine printed text in shades of gray. **IMPORTANT,even though we have attempted to maintain the integrity of the original work, the present facsimile reproduction may have missing letters and blurred pages, poor pictures due to the age of the original scanned copy.** This magazine has been formatted from its original version for publication. Great, but unpretentious, this issue is an extraordinarily rare symbol of what was going on in those early years of the modern UFO phenomena.

Editor
Saucerian Publisher, 2023

The
SHAVER MYSTERY
MAGAZINE

Being dedicated to the further study of the hidden truths as presented in the fact-fiction stories by Richard S. Shaver, made famous in the past three years in AMAZING STORIES magazine.

Subscription Price 50c per Issue

OBTAINED ONLY

THROUGH MEMBERSHIP

THE SHAVER MYSTERY CLUB

CONTENTS

VOL. II   1948   NO. 2

Frontispiece by H. W. MacCauley

Interior Illustration by Virgil Finlay

THE SHAVER MYSTERY MAGAZINE

is Published by

RICHARD S. SHAVER, EDITOR & PUBLISHER

RT. 2 BOX 74, LILY LAKE,
McHENRY, ILLINOIS

❧ EDITORIAL ❧

OUR editorial this month is going to be devoted to a discussion in general of club progress, and bits of news that we feel you as a club member would like to know about. First off, the sensational expose of the flying saucers which was presented in the club magazine last issue, with special permission of FATE magazine, proved to be one of the greatest "proofs" thus far that forces beyond human (the average human) understanding are at work in the "world" around us. We who are interested in the Shaver Mystery, have, of course known this all along. But the flying saucers have furnished us with a *definite* proof.

More than anything else, true, or untrue, it remains a fact that the government is interested in the phenomenon of the flying saucers. It may have no significance, but the fact remains that the Federal Bureau of Investigation has taken the time and trouble to interrogate me on what I know about the flying saucers—and for that matter, about the Shaver Mystery Itself. As I say, this may have no significance, but nevertheless it proves one point: *There are flying saucers. And they constitute a problem that so far our government, or any government, has been unable to resolve to its satisfaction.*

I maintain that the flying saucers are space ships, but apparently the FBI is not of this opinion, or if it is, no definite admission of this belief has been released. But I now pose this question: If the flying saucers are *not* space ships, then what are they? It is all too apparent that they are not a product of the engineering and productive genius of *our* present civilization. If they were they would no longer be a mystery. Also, if they were a product of ours or of some foreign power, the knowledge would be known through any of a number of channels available to all governments. The intense interest in the origin of the flying saucers, therefore leads one to believe that their origin is *not* known. So my contention, in answer to the posed question is that the flying saucers *are* space ships. This I have contended all along, as you club members know. It is my firm belief that the future (near) will bear out my theory as fact.

You will find, to get on to other things, that in coming issues of the club magazine, many interesting articles will be presented. Some of them will be found in this issue, most in others. There is, for example, a transcript of an informal discussion at a famous mid-western University by a group of Professors and students. This discussion concerns the Shaver Mystery—analyzed from the cold, practical viewpoint of modern thinkers. You will read what was discussed yourself, so no need to go into detail on the matter here. Then there is the debate between myself and Robert Kidwell, which originated in AMAZING STORIES, and which is now being presented—this time with the views of Mr. Kidwell in great detail, in the club magazine. There will also be articles on radio-activity, a subject which I feel is of paramount importance to every living being today—for it concerns *you,* and what can and *will* happen unless men come to their senses.

There is of course, "Mandark." We will try and present this to you in its entirety before very long. And there are so many things. The thought is staggering of how much there really is. I wish we could make this little magazine a hundred pages or more each issue. But our club is small, and since we exact no dues the only way we can expand the magazine is to enroll more interested people. You can help in this matter by telling people you know who are interested in *truth* about our club, and getting them to join. In the meantime, rest assured that all the latest information both pro and con, pertaining to any portion of the Shaver Mystery, will be presented to the club as quickly as possible. We've shown we *have* something, and we'll prove that we have more . . . Richard S. Shaver.

READER'S SECTION

Each issue we will publish as many pertinent letters to the Shaver Mystery as space allows. We urge all readers to contribute any facts, personal or otherwise, to help our research.

Dear Mr. Shaver:

I am going to withhold judgment of the whole Shaver Mystery until I know more of the details. However, there are certain matters I wish Mr. Shaver would clear up for me personally right now.

On pages 20-1 of the first issue of the magazine, Mr. Shaver says that while he was serving a term in jail for bootlegging he was visited one night in his cell by the projection of Nydia, who opened his door, hypnotized the prison guard and made him open the outside door of the jail, led Mr. Shaver out of the building and then for several miles deep into a wood, into a case where he remained for about a year, studying the ancient mech and the thought records.

Very well. If we are to take this literally, as the truth, as Mr. Shaver insists, it makes him a jail-breaker!

The next question is: What happened after he came out of the cave later on? Was he rearrested and sent back to serve out his original term? Did he give himself up voluntarily? Or is he still a fugitive from justice?

It seems to me that Mr. Shaver should make this matter absolutely clear, because on the answers to these various questions hinges, to me, the entire veracity of *everything* Mr. Shaver says.

Let me explain: IF Mr. Shaver actually did break out of jail that night and follow this strange woman, as he says, and went with her to the cave, this fact can be proved by investigating Mr. Shaver's criminal record. Breaking jail is a rather serious matter, and if he was in prison for illicit liquor running, as he admits, his case is on record and can be investigated and checked up. So, if he actually did get out, in his physical body, as he stoutly maintains, he was an escaped criminal and as such is known to the police, who can tell us the true story. This will prove his assertion that he did visit the cave under the circumstances given; but it will put him in the odious light of being a jail-breaker at the same time. He should explain.

On the other hand: If the police record should show that Mr. Shaver did not break out of his cell but served his entire term, then the only conclusion to be drawn from his statements are that he is lying, or that he dreamed it all, or that he went to the caves or Lower Astral Realms in his spirit body.

If he is lying about this part of the story, how can we be sure he is not lying about the rest of the story? If he merely dreamed it, the whole Shaver Mystery falls flat and is not worth any more of anybody's time. While if he "went" to the caves in his astral or spirit body, during a trance, then the whole thing becomes an occult matter and must be judged accordingly.

It looks to me as if this is a rather serious matter. Personally, I don't care whether Mr. Shaver broke jail or not; but I do care a great deal about knowing the TRUTH of the matter. And I think all the members of the Club are entitled to an explanation, don't you?

If I had more time and the means I would make it a point to look up Mr. Shaver's criminal record myself; because according to his own statement he went to prison for bootlegging. His present address is known; and whether he is now using his own name or an alia, he can easily be traced, and the truth learned. Someone should do this anyway.

In any event, whether Mr. Shaver broke out in the physical body, or merely went into trances while in prison, he is today an *ex-convict*. Personally, I won't hold that against him; for O. Henry served a term in jail and lived it down successfully; and so do many other individuals, of course. But there may be some readers who will feel that such a person's word cannot be relied upon.

I don't want you to publish this letter; but I really would appreciate Mr. Shaver's explanations of the above questions. Here at last, I believe, is a statment of his which can be proved one way or the other; and it seems to me very important that we know the correct answers before proceeding much further.

If I am mistaken in this myself, please tell me; but I am sure I read the article correctly, for I have it before me right now.

Please understand, my friend; I am not trying to be mean or picky about this; but I do believe Mr. Shaver has not explained himself clearly enough and therefore I would like the

Continued on Page 32

MANDARK

By RICHARD S. SHAVER

Continuing the tremendous 200,000 word Novel
- - - the true story of the Life of Christ

CHAPTER V

AND it became Lila's wish to have Yahveh under her hand, a slave of her pleasures —and into her loneliness blossomed a plan. She did not understand what her Lord was trying to do, did not understand or believe in his ways of thought of his intent of good works for the future of men. To her the race of man was a kind of toy animal, made for her pleasure and profit, and nothing else at all. It deserved no consideration from her and she was sure it would get none. Little love was wasted on her by the increasing number of the followers of Yahveh, who could not understand why he had attached to his person a female of such obviously unvirtuous nature. So she was left to herself for most of the time each day, and only occasionally could she inveigle the young God into her arms for passion's surcease from labor.

The love she bore him did not die, but it shrank and changed under the light of her inherited, biased, devil's reason into another thing; he became a desired thing, a something she wished to humiliate, to make bow down to her, to make to obey even unto death —to make "her" creature utterly.

So it was that Lila took to searching through the largely empty and abandoned laboratories for a certain bottle of the old-time bearing a certain label—for the lore of the caves was one which included centuries of searching such stores and examining the properties of drugs and chemicals they found there, by experiment. And such knowledge of what might be found and what certain strange symbols upon bottles might mean was a lore handed down from witch-mother to imp-son to witch-maid, and many and devious were the uses to which the ancient medicines, aphrodisiacs, and nutrient and medicinal fluids and powders were put by the savage underworld races. For instance, a certain label "ELIXIR" was one greatly sought everywhere in the caverns, for the liquid it contained was so potent for health as to make an old man seem young again.

And finally she found the little brown capsules in the box marked "Nopium"—(cannot opium). For in those days the poppy's gum was not shortened to the name "Opium" (Open your Eyes)—it has made you sleep (meant cannot open your eyes—root meaning).

With the box of potent sleep powders in her hand, the silkenly slithering sandals of Lila whispered back to her place in the sleeping chamber of the young God, her mind a stiff guard against any matching mind. And Lila dressed up her hair with great care, and her body she oiled with sweet perfumed oil of Samarkand, and slipped on the fragile blossom-petal fabrics from the ancient time to stand bewitchingly before Yahveh, dressed like a princess, but with her mind full of a hidden evil resolve.

The giant youth probed her face with his eyes, searching for some change in her which he sensed, but could not fathom.

Above, in Jerusalem, the feast of the passover was come, and Jesus was at the home of Simon the leper.

Yahveh sat to table with Lila Onderde serving his synthetic foods from the ancient stores, and pouring him drinks from the vials of the Gods. (Those liquids and solids known only to modern man by the legendary words "Nectar and Ambrosia"—the Food of the Gods.)

With her back to him and her mind skipping swiftly from elusive image to image so that no guarding ray would watch or catch her thought, Lila dropped a pallet of sleep producing drug into the young God's cup. The deed was done, her father's evil nature had gained the ascendancy over her Yahveh-inspired goodness—but could she carry to fulfillment her long hidden plans?

Soon the great black and beautiful limbs of Yahveh were sprawled in deep slumber on his silken couch in a sleep more profound for the terrible strain of the last years—a strain seldom relieved by natural sleep for him.

WHILE he slept, as was her habitual custom, Lila went to his great long range ray and sent the glittering view-ray, which was also the conductive bearer of many kinds of deadly electric flows when so adjusted—sent the deadly beam sweeping and wheeling along and across the lines of battle. For many months she had thus seized every opportunity so to watch and revel her soul in the terrible scenes of struggle and death—but her purpose had been to accustom the warriors and watch-rays to seeing her at the controls of Yahveh's ray weapons. Usually Yahveh had been there to watch her, and no one had seen any harm in her play.

But this time the ray was not under the hands of Yahveh's loyal Lila. Instead an ambitious woman had seized her first opportunity for assertion of her domination—her will to power had subjugated all love and loyalty to Yahveh within her mind—and as the great ray wheeled and swept in long arcs across the battle field, every man it touched or approached dropped—and no loyal men at the rays still conscious could reach Yahveh's ray—for Yahveh knew better than to set up a ray-field in a way that it could be assaulted by treachery within. This very customary precaution of all ray warfare proved Yahveh's undoing today—for no one could stop the slaughter of the royal troops by the treacherous hand of the Mistress of Yahveh.

As the well-known ray of the Master, Yahveh himself, swept thus in sudden treacherous murder across the beleaguered battle lines—many a worshipper of the might and wisdom of Yahveh looked and cursed him as he died—unknowing what had happened—knowing only that the master had gone mad and was killing them at their posts.

The sweeping search rays* ceased their long, tedious watch arcs, and stopped from their poking and prying along the ways leading into the stronghold of wisdom—and took up instead the auto-movements of short sharp areas of mathematically calculated coverage which they were constructed to make when no hand was at the bar of control.

While Jesus was being betrayed above the surface in Jerusalem, the Messiah of the ancient writings, the true answer to all true ancient prophecy from the Elder God's words —the actual Messiah—was being betrayed by his mistress deep below the soil of Jerusalem.

The whole front line of Yahvey's army (an arc over sixty miles across—long range rays run to sixy miles and more range—penetrating through rock as a knife through butter—and there are those who swear to 125 miles range) fell silent under the traitorous, unexpected fire of Lila from the Master weapons used so long by Yahveh's hands alone (and Lila's only sometimes playfully). Her huge ray swept on out toward the armies of her father, and her thought came to him over the ray—swiftly told him of the turn the war had taken.

Now down upon the suddenly defenseless lines of ray-mech of the loyal warriors of Yahveh came a swift concentration of a multitude of ray beams.

They fell, those helpers of the last true God, like tenpins.

THE Hell of destruction, the cries of his dying men, struck vaguely through Yahveh's sleeping, drugged mind. The great black man raised himself feebly, struggling mightily for consciousness against the drug.

Lila turned to him from the great seat before his weapon board, where the many controls were set in a great intricate bank of switches, dials and levers. She spoke soothing, honeyed, loving words to his drooping, heavy-lidded eyes. But the tones of her voice from which she could not keep some note of exultation sparked within Yahveh a sudden memory of past readings of her mind. His God-swift mind, even in its drugged sleep, could not help relating together the exultation in her voice with his knowledge of her hidden desires . . . Only his defeat could rouse exultation in her—only the coming slavery and debauch of his person to her foul inner lustful desires could cause just those notes in her voice.

Yahveh struggled to his feet, his great body driven by a will that no man living on earth could equal, and struck Lila one blow with the back of his hand. She fell against the far wall and slid to the floor unconscious. He mounted the firing seat of the monstrous engine of destruction which had proved his undoing when Lila got hold of its controls . . . the chief defense of his sanctuary when he was in control . . . And Yahveh fired steadily with a great scythe of destruction leaping out in an arc for a hundred miles across the honey-combing caverns upon the many lines of the advancing armies of Satantes Onderde.

The devils were pushing forward a thousand new weapons, were near his line of defense. They fell now by the hundred, by the thousands, under his terribly accurate fire bolts . . . But the caverns were aswarm with them in all directions, all the many allies Satantes had called in from the farthest caverns—many armies pushed steadily ahead against the terrible fire of this Angel of the Lord—Yahveh the Terrible. From his rear they pushed nearer and nearer unobserved even by Yahveh.

At the last a mass of hundreds of beams of numbing paralysis rays converged at the base of the great lashing column of death-fire that marked the titanic energy source of his weapon's firing beam . . . cut the terrible strength of the dynamos behind it. His mighty brain at last blacked out under the combined irresistible flows of numbing penetrative rays.

Above on the surface . . .

"Art thou the Christ?" asked the High Priest.

And Jesus said, "I am, and ye shall see the son of man sitting on the right hand of power, and coming in the clouds of Heaven."

Jesus was in sore straits above, but had a supreme faith in the might of the invisible, unseen power which had protected and taught him so long.

CHAPTER VI

SATANTES ONDERDE, sitting on his golden chair within the great gloomy chamber called the "torture room," gloated over the bound limbs of the great ebony figure of Yahveh the Terrible.

Yahveh was bound with many wires of the ancient unrusting metal to what had once been an operating table. This place, the torture room, had once been a part of the ancient hospital of that forgotten city of the depths. (This hospital, since the degenerate evil devil-race had no use for such tender thoughts as caring for each other when sick and injured, even their own relatives or friends, had for centuries been used solely for the purposes of prolonged torments. These profound tortures were immensely aided by the medical rays which were used for no other purpose by the stupidity of the Ruler's people. They were especially potent beneficial rays—and would keep a victim alive many lifetimes after he would have ordinarily have died of sheer agony. These rays were so potent that a limb could be severed, replaced and healed together again. Needless to say, torture under these conditions was a vastly more intricate "art" than without the life-prolonging beneficial rays).

Lila had been sent to her former quarters, her father expecting her to take up her former life of obedient child where she had left off. But Lila had drunk of strong waters since she had left her home to follow the lure of the mighty strength and beauty of the son of the Elder Gods—and was no longer content with the role of an obedient child.

Seated in her own rooms before the potent ray-mech with which it was equipped (a mechanism brought specially for her from far-off Tibet and excelled in power only by her father's personal equipment) she swept her master ray down into the room where Yahveh lay bound, stretched by the many wires wound tightly and painfully around and around his body and the great wheeled table. The table had been pushed before Satantes' great golden chair, as was the custom for these frequent entertainments of special invitation.

Yahveh looked calmly with his insupportably brilliant and penetrating gaze—at this slim dark madman who now held his life in his cruel and shapely hands. What Yahveh saw did not reassure him, for there was little in the face—that hook-nosed, weak-chinned, vague-eyed face that attempted to stare down the great spirit of Yahveh.

But Satantes could only flush and lower his own black eyes, with their long girlish lashes, before the simple open scorn in Yahveh's look. This dish of terror on the strength of the dark figure bound before him was too strong for Satantes, he wished heartily the business could be gotten over without his presence, which was for him a most unusual wish. But, then, he reasoned, he did not need to look at the Black Magician's eyes. Satantes waved one jeweled hand, the whole vast room twinkled the light from jeweled ancient pillar to glittering statues' gemmed eyes to the metal fixtures of the time forgotten hospital—and back to glitter again in the stones of the rings on that hand that was bidding a horrible deed be done.

Since Yahveh's eyes were green pools of mighty wisdom, of terrible truth, of vast sanity and clarity—and only an honest and sane man could look into Yahveh's eyes without panic striking into his soul . . .

The mindless grinning slaves of the torture room put out those two terrible eyes of earth's sane man, and Satantes gloated now for he dared to look upon the face of the son of the Gods.

As Satantes sat thus gloating upon the bloody sockets of those terrible eyes—as his face flushed with triumph . . .

LILA Onderde swept her view ray down into the torture room in search of her captured husband—in search of him whose love had not been denied her or away from her for many moons. Her young eyes became suddenly bright as a snake's, and the glitter of death came into them, the wet of her lips became suddenly the dew of venom as she saw what her father had done to her lover and was preparing to do further. And no thought of planning was required of her to remove the only obstacle between her and rule of all Satantes' kingdom, and his wealth that was so much greater than any surface ruler's.

As Satantes thus sat gloating over the doing of his obedient slaves, a great bolt blazed suddenly down from above, from Lila's swift young hands—and her father's yellow teeth bared in a greater grin still as he clutched at his chest where suddenly a great hole had appeared and the blood gushed over his golden and scarlet robe, and pooled at his feet as he tottered and fell scrabbling in the blood from his own breast. The whole room filled with the smell of the burning flesh of his chest, for Lila had made quite sure there would be no mistake about whether he was dead or not. And her voice came after the bolt and told the slaves to stand and move not till she came.

Something within Lila had revolted? No, indeed! She had planned all this very carefully—move by move—as she had hoped it to occur—just what would happen next! She had meant from the first to kill her father after her treachery to Yahveh had placed Yahveh in her power, under her rule—in her hands alone.

But her movements had been obstructed, and her timing confused by the fuss of many slaves, and maiden friends, and other distractions—Satantes had lived a few moments longer than she had planned upon.

She mused, as she sauntered down to the torture chambers—to take her place in her father's great golden chair—which had watched so many good men torn to pieces for his entertainment—to remove the great seal of power from his finger and place it upon her own thumb—"Perhaps it will be safer to have a blind lover than a rebellious and jealous Yahveh watching over me with eyes."

Lila had her will now, those things she had planned and wished for so long had all fallen her way now. The caverns, those known to her—all lay ready for her power to dominate and exact tribute. The mighty Yehveh, the great black-skinned magician, was a blind and helpless man wholly in her hands. She would miss those eyes, she mused— but there were other things in life.

She walked lightly, triumphantly, happily into the torture chamber.

*   *   *   *   *

Now between Lila Onderde and Yahveh, son of Jehovah of Sabaoth, began a strange and terrible struggle that was not to be ended so long as they both had breath.

Lila, making, from habit, with her body those sinuous little movements of her lips and waist and breasts that had first enraptured Yahveh—with her eyes hot upon his blind sockets . . . realized suddenly that the mighty black man would never again see her with his eyes—and that her chiefest weapon against his will—the weapon that had always won for her time to obtain her will in one way or another—her beauty and its effect upon his virility—the lure of her dancer trained body's seductive wisdom—was now gone from her.

Slowly, less happily and gladly, she went and sat upon the great gold chair where her father had sat to enjoy so many prolonged death struggles of so many brave men in the past . . . Went and seated herself upon the chair where it dominated the sightly room of the ancient art of healing that was now so tainted with blood and death of centuries of evil that the odor of an age of agony and butchery hung like a charnel house there. She looked moodily down upon the bound and blinded black body of the mighty young giant where he lay before her on the great wheeled table.

With carefully chosen and honeyed words she sought carefully to acquaint the proud young Godling of his new status. Of her will to have him for her willing slave, and not as any dominating lord of her bed-chamber and her fate at all—of her plans to rule over all the cavern world and over him as well, and her words were these:—"Oh, my Prince of Darkness, how sad it is that I could not kill my father quickly enough to save your eyes. As soon as I might reach a weapon the deed was done, but I was too late. No more can you see my body in the dances you love—no more can you delight in my face that has given you so much joy in the past. But with the mental vision of telaugment mech you may yet see in those other ways that are so vastly more intimate and revealing, so that in truth not much is lost to you—and you can borrow eyes by the use of such mech-ray to see all things. Not much is lost you."

THE young God had only stared at the sound of her honeyed voice with his sightless, bloodily painful sockets, still dripping from the deed, and would not talk to her. She had not unbound him from his place of torment. He had not seen the ray which had killed her father, and if he had, there was no way to know it was her who had killed him—of if she had—knowing her devious mind, he had no way of knowing it was a deed done for love of him. Did she not now inherit all her father's power and wealth? He had not forgotten that she had turned against him and had brought all his life-work to a nothing. He would never forgive her. Finally he made answer:—

"Lila, daughter of evil, whom I have tried to make into a servant of love, tell me this—"Now that you inherit your father's power over these poor mad devils of a people of yours, over these slaves and women and servants of your father's—what do you mean to do with all this inheritance?"

"First, oh my Prince, I mean to make a willing servant of you, so that no more must I wait upon your word—or consider your wishes before my mind dares think of plans or ambitions or pleasures or desires. I will show you the way to mighty empire with that power, but an Empire in which I am the head, and not you. You must answer to me upon your mighty word of honor that you will obey me, that you will strive to make me as great as you could have made yourself great had you thought and planned as I would have thought and planned—or as you would now have become but for my father's savage warring against you. You must admit once and for all that I am the ruler, and you the obedient servant of my power. I must have your word, for I know that your pledge is the strongest tie by which I could bind you, mightier to you than chains of dungeons. I do not mean to let this power I have acquired be given over to you—for I am a wayward woman and you might one day be angry with me and put me aside."

But young Yahveh, sorrowing for his eyes that were gone, and filled with a terrible God-anger against the stupidity and evil of this woman that had frustrated all his plans for the future—would not give Lila Onderde, the daughter of King Satantes, any promise of any kind.

Now Lila sought to frighten him by putting the torturers again to work upon the mighty male beauty of his body that lay naked before her in his majesty, a terrible tower of dark strength fallen before here evil will. And a great fear of him struck deep into her evil soul, and that fear became resolve to make this man something that could never hurt or avenge his God-anger upon her.

The young Godling, bemused with many thoughts of all that had so abruptly ended his efforts toward supremacy to regenerate the human race with the ancient wisdom—with the darkness of blindness and pain concealing the purpose of the many hands about him—did not resist in any way. When the pain struck into his mind, he succeeded in killing two of the many slaves with blows of his head. Lila laughed shrilly at his futile struggles to break the wires that bound him, and gasped a little with fear of the terrible strength that had slain two of her slaves before her eyes even though he was bound.

Now they kept on under her orders, gave him slight cuts with the knives, and little searings with the red hot irons, to show him what might happen to him who should resist the will of the new ruler, but he paid no attention to them. Yahveh only stared upward toward space with his sightless eye-sockets and filled his mind with the complete realization that this was his first genuine understanding of all earthmen's despair. For now he knew that there was truly no hope for men to progress ever upon this evil planet turning under this evil sun. And he understood why the Elder race had fled from the sun so fearfully. And he knew what Lila would do—and prayed silently she would do it swiftly.

Slowly a burning insane anger—the heritage of her evil and tainted family, began to flame terribly within Lila's veins, and the fire flamed higher and higher against this stubborn black giant who would not acknowledge her as the dominant one.

"Who then was this black giant who would not acknowledge her, would do nothing but refuse her every wish, yet expected of her such serviture as he would not give himself

—such submission as was required only of slaves. He should find out who Lila Onderde was, he should crawl at her feet yet."

At Lila's angry words and shouted orders, obedient to her flaming eyes now bent over the blind giant's face, obedient to her gesturing wild hands that beat in anger upon Yahveh's chest—fearful of Lila, the daughter, even more than they had been of her Father—and even more than the superstitious fears they bore toward this terrible son of the darkness, this creature of the night, this mighty black warrior from no one knew where—Lila's slaves began a more serious torture of Yahveh, to break him to Lila's will.

YAHVEH'S mighty muscles bound his great body in an armor of swift and terrible force, a rippling black armor that gave fear to any man who looked upon it—for it was super-human strength.

So they cut through those mighty God-muscles one by one—slow cutting, drawing the ragged knife edges deliberately through the gaping terrible wounds—slowly and agonizingly till the steel grated on the bone.

The slaves not doing the terrible work suitably, and not getting from Yahveh's trained nerves and terrible will more than groans of anguish—Lila suddenly took the tools from their hands in a fury and sent them all from her sight. She remained, gazing upon the wreck of the mighty beauty she had worshipped, now seen through a haze of hate and frustrated anger.

That was a gloomy chamber, that past place of god-like mercy when it was the home and hospital of the Elder Race—now to see the last son of the Elder Race, his black and beautiful form a wreck and an evil deed forever there in that place.

That spirit that is mother Earth—that is called "Tithea," came softly through the rock walls weeping, and tried to touch Lila's heart with her misty fingers, and leaned over the bloody Yahveh's still form and kissed him gently—and went away weeping to that place that is every-where-under-earth to sleep and weep again and sorrow away the years that must pass before earth's last agony is reached.

For that was a place where she had wept often and where many another brave man had given up his all to avoid one slight additional agony before death.

Now Lila spoke to Yahveh, striving to hold her flaming anger from her words—saying "Oh, my Yahveh, give me one small promise that you will not work against me, that you will not try to avenge yourself upon me—and we will let time cure the anger between us and the differences that have brought us to this pass."

But Yahveh scorned her with words—saying: "Wanton, faithless, foolish one, life is no longer desirable to me—with you or without you. You could never understand what I think."

And the terrible anger again flamed through all Lila's body, and her veins were liquid fire, and her hands seemed alive with hate, and she went on with the terrible work. The scorn he held for her was seen by Lila, and this knowledge burned away the love she had had for him to the last part—nothing lived within Lila Onderde but the flaming spirit of evil which she had inherited. And always as she worked, she asked—shrilly or mutteringly—"Yield to me your word of honor that you will uphold me, will be my liegeman."

But Yahveh only stared at her blazing mad beauty with his sightless empty sockets and smiled a strange sad smile and did not even groan, now. For pain can deaden the nerves—or Yahveh set his will against the feeling of pain.

The tower of dark strength she had loved became under her hands a blood-sodden wreck, a swiftly dying man. And the day dragged on and still Lila labored and racked her brains for ways to hurt, to agonize this giant of stubbornness. And she found not any in her memory of all the many tortures and devices for wringing pain from the victims were effective against Yahveh's will.

For Yahveh knew well her nature, and that now she had turned entirely from his way, from his teachings, now that she had let her evil nature rule her entirely there was nothing she would not do—no evil thing from which she would withdraw.

And whether all these evils Lila did that day and later were her own will or from some subtle synthetic will-ray from a far dero-ray man, we will never know. The record did not show that.

Or perhaps it was Yahveh's will not to live any more under the domination of an evil will, for that would be the way of true logic—now that failure seemed to claim all his hopes, it may be that the God-logic of his record training indicated that the only hope for life lay in not allowing his Divine Elder wisdom becoming the property and use of Evil ray rule by control—which he foresaw would be his fate.

Yahveh did think now that the race of men were doomed no matter how many Yahvehs might labor on earth to turn back the tide of evil degeneration that was swallowing forever all the clean spirit of man inherited from his mighty ancestors and leaving instead a man that was less than an animal for stupidity by the Titan standards—and an animal whose nature was less than the wild creatures, being so very evil where they were evil only by necessity. Whatever Yahveh thought during those hours of his torment, while above in Jerusalem for his disciple Jesus of Nazareth, the trail was shortening to the cross—we do know that the centuries to come after him were even darker and more terrible for all mankind than those that had gone before. And we know that today the atomic bomb has set the scene for even greater degradation and destruction of all mankind everywhere. It may be that his great wisdom foresaw all these things and bade him die now, instead of suffering on under Lila Onderde's evil sway.

WHEN the time of sleep had come again, and passed a half away—up above on the surface where the moon glowed softly over the hideous burnt desert, and over the man-built "glory" of Jerusalem the "golden"—that had always looked to the God-taught Yahveh like the made dreams of sterile pygmies worked out in stone and mortar—then Lila desisted at last from her labor, from her terrible labor of madness and rage and stupidity—from her labor of suddenly inverted "love."

Lila went and sat again upon the lovely ancient golden chair of her father's that had been his father's and had once belonged to a child of the Elder race—and she sat and looked upon the thing that had been the man she loved more than riches or her father's palace, once—long ago when she had gone through the perilous caverns to be at his side. She looked upon the great black body that was now stripped of all strength and beauty and left a horrifying bloody wreck upon the table. And she looked dull-eyed at her red-dripping hands, and at her white arms that were blood-dabbled to the shoulders.

Never again, she thought savagely, albeit wearily, would those mighty thews carry that gigantic body about under the stim-beam augment rays so swiftly that the eye could not follow his movements—never again would those swift hands upon a ray control best an army of lesser men with slower hands.

Lila wept, and bent her beautiful and now openly evil face toward him, her wild hair streaming madness about her naked shoulders, her hands all bloody clots—her white arms splashed with his life-blood she stretched toward him—and she asked him in a childish voice from which all the wily feminine magic was gone forever for him—saying foolishly, pleadingly—"Yield thou thy will, My Yahveh!"

But Yahveh lay motionless and did not move, for he had been unconscious for a long time—though moaning and twisting steadily. The binding straps and wire now held uselessly his mighty limbs, since the muscles were for the most part cut through, and his life was nearly bled away, and still bleeding slowly through the great wounds.

And as Yahveh lay thus near death, he heard the voice faintly and far away, and felt a great relief that he would no longer have to serve his sense of duty to men against the hopeless cause—to repair all the damage done by time and the evil sweep of the terrible de-magnetic from the sun to this abandoned pitiful remnant of a great race, the cast-off children of an ill-conceived experiment of the long gone fathers of all men.

And the weakness of death came upon Yahveh, and he slept.

But the red and evil madness had left Lila's brain for a time. Something like the spirit of the girl who had wilfully left the ease of her soft couch in Satantes' palace and gone like a moth to the mighty flame of male life that was Yahveh, the young and mighty magician from the depths of the mystery of the caverns—the terrible warrior who could defy the whole army of her father's ray fighters and live on and laugh at them—came again to Lila and the weeping made her heart soft again for a time.

Lila Onderde rose from the chair, sobbing like a child, and pushed the wheeled table slowly across the floor. Under one of the ancient miraculous healing lamps she pushed the now quiet body, and closed about herself and him the insulating walls of the chamber that keep the healing rays from escaping—reflect the benecial rays back again and again upon the tortured body, so that a ray pressure of a very beneficial nature was built up inside.

There, where no one could see her kindness which was so unnatural to the race of people under Jerusalem—she bound up his wounds with cloths torn from her skirts—and went and left him under the healing lamp.

(And it may be that that kindness was the subtle spirit that is Tithea*, our mother Earth, working her sweet will through the woman's body. And it may well be that there is no such spirit as Tithea, or any spirit of any kind on this dull earth—but only men like you and I and sometime in the future, if we try—like Yahveh again. For such is my belief).

* * * * *

LILA went now sorrowfully to her bed and left the great black mystery of Yahveh, the Messiah, within the healing chamber, the beneficial lamps burning warmly about him. The day came again, and the great, nearly empty castle that was before Satantes'—is now Lila's—slept the morning away.

When the sun was midway of the sky, and the telerays brought its light into the caves—Lila rose and ate a cheerless meal. Then she went alone down to the torture room that was again for a time being used for what it was made for—to bring the sick back to health again. And she looked in upon the great man's wracked and wrecked body and love struck her—she said to Yahveh—"Oh, My Prince, turn your ways from their mystery and your heart toward me again, and we will yet rule together over all the vast underwold."

But Yahveh, whose wounds had closed and nearly healed again under the mighty magic of the healing rays of the ancient wisdom, only shook his head and wearily closed his eyes.

Suddenly, inexplicably, the red rage burned again within Lila, for she perceived only that Yahveh scorned and despised her, and saw no good in her offer of herself to him, of her good body to his wrecked and now ugly one—and that under any conditions other than his own choosing he would have none of her—thought of herself as a despised convenience to Yahveh—and "Hell hath no fury like a woman scorned,—nor serpent venom!"

This man whom she thought had loved her should refuse even to pretend for a moment that she might be the dominant one and himself the slave. Lila, still only a savage child in the mind, and of no true development—could still see no other explanation in Yahveh's refusal of her as the ruler of her father's kingdom. She did not realize that in Yahveh's logical mind, a person once evil is never again a friend. A double-cross could never be wiped out by any promise or words or even actions. She did not realize that he thought of her only as a mad woman whom he could not now understand how to placate—could not comprehend any more than a man tries to comprehend the vagaries of the ripples of cross-winds on water. (For the vagaries of an evil nature to be figured out by a logical mind was to Yahveh very simple—it would always work out to an evil end if the motivation sprang from a mind tainted with the sun polarity and inductive of the disintegrant forces that cause evil will.)

For Yahveh thought of her only as a mad woman with whom there was no way for logic to bargain or to reason about anything, for she had failed to remain loyal to him after he had demonstrated to her that he trusted her. For Yahveh there was no more to be said between them, for logic does not say that an evil person may be allowed to live at

---

In space are ethereal spirits, many kingdoms of them, just as described in Ohaspe and many another book—but they may none of them come near this earth because of our sun. For the body of a spirit, an etherean, is so slight, of such tenuosity, that the terrible ray flows of destructive energy upon earth and in the spaces around our sun for light years away—tear and burn the sweet ethereal bodies of those we call Peri's, and by many another name.

But once this was not true of earth, and so we have the legends of spirits, and some of those oldest legends are true—for spirits of great tenuosity can live in space which is clean of detrimental electric, which contains only supportive energies which keep their fragile bodies intact. And so it is.

And men say that Tithea, Mother Mu, the very rocks of our earth contain a spirit who is protected from the sun by the insulative rocks—and that this spirit tries and strives always to raise a race of superior being who will fulfill her possibilities for immense immortal life as the spirit of a planet, the God of all the earth. But our stupidity and the terrible destructive radioactive energy atoms from the sun which shower ever a rain of fire upon the surface of earth, keep her surface parts blind and unable to help us as she could if she could know better what we need. But none know how to speak with her but some despised mystics and conjurers of her beloved jungles, and deeper caverns.

all where they may do harm to anything. Only in some unbreakable prison may evil be allowed to have life. (And I hope that is not the true reason why we are too stupid to conquer space travel—that the cold logic of some God-race thought does not forever condemn sun-planet life to the confines of these terrible sunburned worlds—because such—to their minds—may not rise above evil—can't.)

In Yahveh's education from the ancient records there was indicated death for Lila—or a cage for the rest of her life.

So it was that Lila called again the torturers* from their places, and the table was wheeled out—the irons heated in the great brazier before the golden chair. The flaming-faced Lila Onderde took her place again where her father had sat, to watch what might yet be done to this stubborn captive to break that awful will forever to her use.

Yahveh's bones were a mighty and beautiful framework to hold up the God-life in him. But at Lila's burning, hissing words they took their tools and slowly, one by one and little by little these zombie-like automatons took their awful tools and carefully and religiously broke Yahveh's bones one by one, crushing them inch by slow inch while Lila still kept shrieking her useless question—"Yield, stubborn fool, yield me now?"

But Yahveh did not bother answering a "maniac," not understanding how any answer might help him anyway—for such is wisdom that it cannot comprehend a great depth of stupidity any more than stupidity can comprehend the vastness of reason—the devious ways of mad minds being a mystery to wise men always—while to the mad and evil nature, the ways of wisdom are equally mysterious and hard to understand. Yahveh only moaned and frothed at the mouth, and rolled feebly about the table with the few sinews that were left to him, the rest of his sundered muculature jerking and jerking in futile attempted movement—and struggled thus futilely against the straps and cutting wires that had bound him so long. Involuntarily he struggled for the life that his reasoning mind told him quite clearly was valueless to him or to her now.

And so his bones were broken, each of them crushed slowly along the whole length, and the work went on the whole day. When night fell, and darkness came and the upward pointing, light-bringing rays were shut off—and the moon far above on the surface of the green earth came out, and the green earth became a misty blue loveliness—still these things labored to make a mighty mind understand what no man of sane mind ever understood—how to get along with evil people. Or how to make him understand he must serve minds less than his own, and that for ends which were to him the opposite of value of goal. And at last they were through and unconsciousness came to Yahveh, and he could no longer moan or writhe.

Lila sat upon her lonely, lovely golden chair, and the moon was brought down to her on the great televisor screen before her—and silvered all her lovely lines and hanging, curling tresses and soft-breasted womanliness of her—and her red-rimmed eyes that looked out of her evilly contorted face upon the wrecked thing, the mangled ugliness that she had made of the mighty man who had loved her beauty and the life that she might have become if the seed of madness and evil had not been so strong within her.

This man had still loved her but a few days ago, and this man she still loved in the weird jungle of madness her mind was swiftly becoming. And again she took the wheeled table on which lay her hopes for greatness and her happiness, and pushed it through the opening into the healing chamber—and closed the walls about him, and again she turned on the great healing lamps electric. And again she went to her bed alone. She was slowly realizing that her will was not great enough to make evil deeds become of value—for she saw that in her first use of power she had robbed herself of everything she most desired

---

(*These things that resembled men such as we call "Nazis" today—these things that obeyed Lila Onderde because she could hurt them—and because their minds had for many generations been partially removed by the ancestors of Lila—by the process called "cutting" which is done with a needle of hot ray that penetrates the skull and cuts only where the two beams meet—) (one who knows of the survival of these terrible ancient arts of evil within the cavern world wonders if there were not some of Lila's stripe still the driving force behind the Hitler mind.)

on earth. But the evil* stupidity that had usurped the tiny place in her mind where self-rule lives, wept itself to sleep nor learned anything from her fool's work. (Nor can evil people ever learn by such things.)

NOW Lila went on with the healing work without more torture for the blasted form of Yahveh. It took a long time. Yahveh lived still, and still laughed sometimes at her for not getting his greatest treasures from him as she wished—for he alone of all life on earth knew the ancient lore and secrets of science.

Lila read the scornful silent laugh in his mind, and put a ray-augment upon his head to see what the whole thought might be that made him laugh so at her. And somehow Lila was surprised to find there still the great being, enthroned within his own mind, who had ruled her so long and still now would not accept her rule.

Without his knowledge of the chemicals and materials of the antique laboratories—of the mysterious and miraculous equipment in the endless warrens of the ancient cities—without his knowledge of the language in whicff the great old thought-records were symboled and the mighty metal books were inscribed—she knew there was no other could read the "magic books",—no other mind, no living man, but only Yahveh on earth could read those mighty secrets. She knew she was as nothing to what she could be if she could win these mental treasures from him.

But now again the swift miraculous flows of antique healing energy from the great hospital lamps made the raw flesh heal back over the unending wound that was Yahveh's crippled body—had been his glory and was now his horror and his sorrow. The crushed bones slowly knit in twisted, shortened shapes of hideous appearance.

Lila fed the bundle of pain till it was well and could think swiftly once again as before without agony wrenching all his mind.

For Lila had still mighty plans for the use of the terrible and powerful, the all-wise mind of this man she could not conquer. When he was as well as he would ever be again, she put the rays from a great master's mechtelaug (a special machine for the careful and multiple augmentation of many thoughts, many trains of thought simultaneously, so that the deepest, most hidden information stands out revealed against all the hiding evasive thoughts—a telepathic augmentation with a multiple detector device of many little rays which simultaneously augment all the various source areas of the brain and all the many various thought flows. But only the Elder race had minds of such capacity that they had need of this device, and Lila thought she had surprised the thought of its use within the mind of Yahveh.) She put the multiple rays upon Yahveh's head and prepared herself to spend a long time, many weeks and months, learning what she thought she must know to fulfill her plans.

Above, in Jerusalem the "golden," the hideous farce of the Crucifixion was playing to a close—and at last Christ died, crying aloud to his father who had deserted him—that mighty figure of transparent black beauty which the projection rays had brought to him so often during the days of his study—"Eloi, Eloi, Lama sabacthani," which later days may have translated aright as to mean "My God, My God, why hast thou forsaken me?"

(And to those who know the caverns—we know that when Christ died, below him

---

For evil is not thought, but a usurpation of the power of thought by a greater power of electric flow than the cells can generate—evil is an inversion of thought—love is always hate in evil minds—and all other things invert likewise in proportion when evil takes over the mind. This whole race under Jerusalem suffered from the infection of disintegrance which is called evil for want of a greater knowledge about it. For evil is sun-polared matter in the brain and they acquired it by using apparatus which they had used to bring sunlight down through the rock into the caverns—the penetrative ray-mech that they used in night time to watch the surface and the far cavern ways for danger—and the watching had given them sun-polared matter by infection—just as radioactivity infects even the dust in the room where there is radio-activity. (Evil can be hereditary, can affect even the inmost chromosomes of the cells—but there is a treatment for it—the direction of a flow of will toward those centers to re-polar the cells naturally—or the direction of a flow of synthetic body electric along those paths of the mind by ray toward where evil is detected by a polarity needle set to distinguish between sun and earth polarity—both of these flows—natural and synthetic can be made to rectify the evil cells into good earth induction again—and the miracles of conversion are these—they have learned to will themselves good again.)

many good people died in torments with the true Messiah—or else that crucifixion never had taken place. For Christ could never have survived or done his work without the help all such work needs today still against the evil ray.) It was truly a dark day for the world when the light and wisdom of the underworld below Jerusalem died of the onslaught of the rods (dero).

And Yahveh's crushed bones slowly knit again in twisted shortened shapes of hideous and evil appearance. His great black body was no longer like a God's—but rather like that which has been pictured by Medievals as the Devil's own twisted and limping form of blackness.

Now from her use of very complex ancient telaugment multiplex beams upon Yahveh's head, to which she had prepared herself to listen very carefully for many, many weeks—occurred a thing which Lila had not expected—but which Yahveh had foreseen when he allowed Lila to "catch" him thinking of the telaugmentplex. Lila was not over wise in the ways of these more intricate machineries, having only the little practical knowledge of it she had learned from her father, which was knowledge handed down from many generations of people who used the machinery, but did not study or learn a great deal more than pushing this-or-that button did this-or-that thing with the mech.

The mighty brain of the young God, having maneuvered Lila into a position where his augmented thoughts had become vastly stronger than Lila's listening thought—suddenly reached out through the wires and little carrier beams of te-rays, through all the many augments his will reached out suddenly and seized upon Lila like a great invisible many-armed monster of strength. So that where Lila had expected to augment all the little thoughts of the young God to great strength so that he might not hide any wisdom from her, her own mind's thought-flows were suddenly and completely overwhelmed—the great strength of the augmentation made his heard thought so strong to her that she could not help but obey him as would a robot, her self being overwhelmed by the vast flow of meaning from the augmentative orifices of the ray mech.

So it was that Yahveh now took command of the terrible kingdom of Onderde. The black and bloody rule of the Onderdes came suddenly to an end. (Satantes is a name not to be confused with the Satan—is a common name—another form of Satan—and Satan is a common name in the caverns—as is John on the surface.)

So it was that Lila Onderde became to the immobile cripple of a God a mental slave so long as he chose to keep the augmentive mech in operation. And Yahveh did not choose to shut the machine off again.

Like a slave, Lila obeyed him now, compelled by the nature of the machine, she herself had set in operation. And because it seemed to be still Lila giving the orders (and whom the people knew to be ruler now), it was Lila moving about and operating the many machines and ray-mech of the private armament of Satantes—while the young God lay still broken and helpless within the healing mech—the other Devils of the tribe paid no attention.

THE young God by mental control made Lila turn on the penetrating beams of beneficial rays, and made them sweep upward through the rock and into the tomb of the Jesus who had died upon the cross. And after a time the vitalizing rays had healed the body, still warm from the slow death of the cross—and Jesus breathed again within the dark sepulchre. For such is the virtue and nature of these rays, they supply the life cells with the activating currents of body electricity, (synthetically,) which cause life to be—until the dead cells again take up the work of making their own electricity.

They are synthesized vital electric, of the same kind as the flesh cells of the body and nerves manufacture, and it is true that they can make a man live again if he be not too long dead. (But so can our own doctors—up to twelve minutes after death.) And Yahveh was still healing himself within the healing-ray chamber, and Christ just placed within the sepulchre when Yahveh forced Lila by his mind's augmented will to turn the great beneficial rays upward upon the still warm corpse. For Yahveh loved Jesus like a son, and for three days the mighty antique magic of life-electric raced upward over the conductive penetrative rays through the rock and into the dead body, making it live in spite of death, and upon the third day Jesus began to breathe of his own will again.

And Yahveh caused Lila to make a picture of a dread angel from a projection of a thought-record of the ancient winged race of winged men of the Planet Hevi-Enn to appear to the watchers who guarded Jesus' tomb. They fled. And Jesus got up from the rock sepulchre, and walked again among men. But the heart of Jesus could not fill with love for his fellow men who had slain him, even though it was the Sadducees—(the Jewish-Roman Quislings) who had caused his death. Jesus lived in secrecy from the Roman government for some time, and eventually Yahveh found a way of bringing Jesus to the underworld of darkness and magic forgotten machinery—and Jesus learned that "his father's house had," indeed, "many mansions."

(Jesus formed, later, one of the many groups of ray people who go about down there, trying always to do good work with the ray mech's might and to make of life in the upper world what it should be—and frustrated always by the devil (dero) race—the degenerate men who cannot think anything but evil always. Still today such groups with the same purposes as Jesus live down there and keep up the struggle against the stupid enemies of life who wish to keep it all secret from the men of the surface—and so far it seems the evil has succeeded and the good failed.)

Now after releasing Jesus from the power of death, the young God Yahveh lay for a long time—long weeks in the healing rays, hoping for good strength to come again into his broken body.

But it came now very slowly, and he could do but little organization work with the services of the desperate Lila, for she struggled always to release herself from his mind's command.

Too, afar off, a young dero of Lila's acquaintance, one who had known her from a child on, and who held a kind of twisted love for her beauty—sat and played always a detrimental ray upon the body of Yahveh unperceived by him—for he saw what Yahveh had done to take command of her. He knew that the mental master of the telaug hook-up was Yahveh, and that he had Lila in his power so long as he could keep his weakened, crippled body awake. The devil knew that she must do as Yahveh willed. So, invisibly diffuse and mild, but steady and unremitting, he played day after day his detrimental weapon ray upon the body of the young God where he lay and struggled against weakness and against sleep—the ray going invisibly through the rock walls of the many great old dwellings and borings and burrows and railroad tubes and vast underground highways, through the endless blanket of gray dust over all the vast beauty of the handiwork of the mighty elder race, through the great vaults of the storerooms where lay piled centuries' accumulations of fabulous treasures and mysterious and magical weapons and mighty stim pleasure machines—and through the luxurious palace of the dead Satantes. And strength at last left Yahveh from this insidious sapping from afar—(and even as I write the same kind of sapping is going on, on my and many another worker's body from afar underground—for the devil race does not change—and still sits and gibbers down there and tries always to keep good from being dominant anywhere) and weakness overcame the mighty crippled God, and he fell asleep.

While he slept, Lila Onderde was released from the grip of the augmented rays of the mech-telaug, and the thunder of Yahveh's mighty ruling thought through her brain dwindled to a gentle murmur as of a sleeping, quiet sea—and Lila with great effort went and took the helmet of the mech-telaug off the God-like head of the black giant.

Now Lila reversed all the connections of the apparatus, for she had learned a great trick from this—to her—chance occurrence, from this sudden domination of her mind by Yahveh, and was now aware of a way of obtaining her goal of complete domination and subjection of Yahveh to her will forever.

TO BE CONTINUED NEXT ISSUE

At the completion of the main part of "MANDARK" there will follow over 50,000 words of proof of this thought-record in the form of footnotes, Biblical, and Historical References -- as important as "MANDARK" itself.

UNIVERSITY ROUND TABLE
ON THE SHAVER MYSTERY

FOLLOWING is a transcript of two round table discussions among the faculty of a mid-western university. Due to the nature of the subject, they have requested that their names be withheld. They are, however, all competent in their respective fields, and represent the sciences of psychology, medicine, biology, science, physics, literature, and ancient history. The moderator and discussion leader is identified by the letter 'M'. The other five members of the group by the figures 1 to 5, inclusive.

* * * * *

(M) Our subject is the so-called Shaver Mystery; the claims expounded by one Richard Shaver in a series of stories which he has written. The stories are written as fiction, but Mr. Shaver claims that they are based upon fact, and that the persons, things, and events he pictures are either actual or typical. He has gained quite a following. Many of the students have expressed considerable interest in it, and I believe that some of the faculty are also quite interested, altho not so openly as the students. We, therefore, decided that it might help clear the thinking on the subject to discuss it, and point out the fallicies, if any. Mr. Shaver's publisher says that he holds proof of Shaver's claim but, to date, has not made it public. Under these circumstances, all we can do is to examine each point by straight logic, and try to determine the probabilities. You gentlemen have all been given advance copies of Mr. Shaver's claims, but, in order to make the record complete, I shall try to outline them as briefly as possible.

Shaver's contention is that, in far pre-historic times, when our solar system was young, the earth was inhabited by a race of super-beings who came here from another solar system. He identifies them as the Elder Race, or, sometimes, as the Elder Gods, altho the term is not used in its theological sense. Altho they were not truly immortal, they had discovered how to prolong their lives almost indefinitely. This, and their highly developed science, seemed so miraculous to the early humans that they were regarded as gods, and the designation is continued by Shaver in order to more easily connect them with various myths.

The mechanical devices of the Elders, which Shaver calls 'mech', were almost everlasting. With various rays, they could scan, or televise, over great distances, project thought and three-dimensional images, kill or destroy, extract thought from another person's mind, or implant thought into it, stimulate any of the emotions, and cure various diseases. Other 'mech' could automatically make food, clothing, or any other article which they might need.

In time, Shaver tells us, the nature of our sun changed. At first, its radiations had been beneficial. Now they also contained detrimental rays which shortened the life-span by causing premature aging, and other ill effects. To escape this, the Elder Race went deep underground, where the solar rays could not penetrate. They constructed huge tunnels and caverns, disintegrating the rock with their rays. Here they built their cities, duplicating the beneficial rays of the sun with their mech, but excluding detrimental rays.

On the surface, the native human race, the Homo Sapiens, had evolved. The solar rays had stunted their growth, and shortened their life to its present span. The gods, particularly the lesser ones, seem to have had quite human emotions and foibles, and to have varied greatly in morality and intelligence. In general, they regarded the surface dwellers with contempt, much as we regard the natives of darkest Africa. Some of the more humane among them did help these early humans in various ways, and the ancient myths and legends are supposed to be the surface peoples version of their activities.

Meanwhile, the Elders had been searching for a more suitable home, one where the sun was beneficial and they could live on the surface. One was eventually found in a far-distant star system. Due to the great distance and the limited transport, they could not take their mech with them. Its location and operation was known only to the higher gods. One of these wanted to make it available to the surface dwellers, but the others did not consider them worthy of it. After a struggle, of which the myth of Prometheus is said to be the surface peoples' version, the humane gods were overwhelmed. The most important mech was hidden and sealed against the possibility that they might some day return to the earth, and the gods left for their new home.

It was not possible to take all of their race with them. Some of the lesser ones were left behind in the caverns. Freed from the restraint of their leaders, some of the lower of them now sank into the depths of depravity. Some of the hidden mech was found, and its use partially discovered by experiment. Various groups began to turn the rays to the surface, bringing in the detrimental solar radiations in a greatly magnified form. This, together with certain radiations caused by the unskilled use of the mech, destroyed a certain part of their brain, and produced a very dangerous form of hereditory insanity.

THESE insane cavern dwellers, whom Mr. Shaver calls 'deros', are completely devoid of any moral sense or humane instinct. As normal persons will, by instinct, usually tend to do good, the deros will, by instinct, try to do harm at every opportunity, and derive great sadistic pleasure from the sufferings of others. With their tamper rays, they cause as much trouble among the surface dwellers as possible. When they can secure the necessary victims, who are usually surface people lured into the caverns, they indulge in unspeakable sadistic orgies. Details of some of these horrors filtered back to the surface, and are said to be the foundation of the devil, hell, and underworld legends of the ancient peoples. The damage which the deros do is fortunately limited somewhat by their lack of skill in using the mech, and by saner and more moral groups. These groups are generally more skillful in the use of the mech, and much more intelligent than the deros. Due to the manner in which the defense mech is placed, they can easily defend themselves from the deros, but cannot completely liquidate them. Some groups have friendly feelings toward the surface dwellers, but hold to the ancient taboos against sharing the mech with them.

Besides these two groups, bands of surface dwellers seem to have found their way into unused parts of the caverns from time to time. They found a safe refuge from their enemies, and the means of a fairly easy living, and remained. The descendents of some of these groups offer no threat so long as they are not interfered with. Others medieval lord and serf relationship. Some of the lords treat their people humane, accord- use the rays for evil purposes when it serves their ends to do so, but do not have the insane urge to kill and destroy which the deros have. The usual social order is the medevial lord and serf relationship. Some of the lords treat their people humane, according to their standards, while other groups are subjected to great oppression.

I speak of these groups in the present tense because it is Shaver's contention that they still live there, with much of the cavern system and most of the mech still intact. He claims that some of these cavern dwellers are in contact with him, by means of rays which he calls 'telaug', and that he has actually seen the mech in operation.

Some of the Elder race in the caverns have solved the secret of some of the more complicated mech, and have become 'gods' themselves. The lesser among the cavern dwellers live in squalor, despite their wonderful mech. They either have not found, or are unable to operate, the mech which would supply them with the necessities of life. Having very little mechanical ability of their own, they can make these things only on the crudest scale, if at all.

In former times, an extensive trade was carried on between the caverns and the surface. Simple articles, either taken from the Elder storehouses or made with their mech, were traded for food, clothing, and other things needed in the caverns. As communications on the surface increased, the danger of discovery became greater for the cavern dwellers, and the trade dwindled. At the present time, trade is a mere trickle.

Even the most friendly among the cavern dwellers are determined to maintain the secrecy of their caverns, and the secrets of their mech. Shaver believes, however, that there is a chance to secure some of their mech, mainly of a medical nature, in exchange for the things which they so desperately need from the surface. His sole interest, he claims, is to arouse sufficient interest, belief, and pressure on responsible groups and agencies, to bring this about.

Mr. Shaver presents his case in several fairly long stories. It is somewhat difficult to condense it into a short summary, as I have tried to do. I have tried to do it fairly. If you believe that I have gone astray in any particular, you are, of course, at liberty to correct me. As I understand it, that is the essence of the Shaver Mystery. Is it a mystery, or it is a hoax? That is the question.

DOCTOR (1), I understand that some of your students have been in correspondence with Mr. Shaver, and that you have studied his replies. How does he appear to you as a psychologist? What can you tell us of Shaver, the man?

(1) First of all, Mr. Moderator, there is a third possibility which you have omitted in stating the case. Mr. Shaver might be entirely sincere, but might be suffering from a delusion.

Considering first the possibility of hoax, it must be remembered that Mr. Shaver is an author. It would be in his interest to make his work produce as large an income as possible. The greater interest he can arouse in his stories, the greater the financial return to both himself and his publisher. His claims of authenticity have aroused a great deal of interest and support. The motive for perpetuating a hoax is clearly present, but it must be remembered that motive is not proof of guilt. That must be determined by the evidence.

Against this, I have only my personal impressions. He impresses me as being honest and sincere—a man who feels that he has a mission in life. Whether this sincerity is based upon fact or delusion could be determined only by a very complete psychoanalysis. I would not commit myself on the basis of the present evidence. He is obviously above the average intelligence, but this would not necessarily be inconsistent with certain psychopathic conditions.

The remaining possibility, that it might be true, can only be proven, in the absence of material evidence, by eliminating the other possibilities. We are obviously unable to do this, and our conclusions, therefore, can only be comparative, and not decisive.

I do believe that the literary worth of Mr. Shaver's stories would have a bearing on the possibility of hoax. I should like to hear an analysis, based only upon literary values, and disregarding the truth or falsity of the claims, from my old friend, Doctor (2).

(2) By comparison with the classics, Mr. Shaver's stories are not masterpieces. By comparison with contemporary fiction, they are very well written. He has a vivid and realistic manner of expression which holds reader interest. The theme of his stories is one which many people would consider too fantastic to be worthy of their time. Amazing Stories, his publisher, is not usually regarded as being among the more respectable or responsible publications. Were it not for these two facts, I believe that he would be well up among the popular fiction writers. If it is a hoax, I consider it a foolish one, because I believe that he could earn an even greater income by using more conventional themes, and dealing with a better accepted publisher.

(3) I should like to point out that the premise in the latter part of Doctor (2)'s statement would be true if it were a hoax. However, if it is true, or if Mr. Shaver believes it is true, then the vividness and realism could easily be dependent upon this. One can always write more convincingly if they themselves are convinced. If this should be the case, then he might be a very mediocre writer on more conventional themes.

(M) I think that Mr. Shaver's space ships should have a priority in our discussion. This Elder Race is supposed to have come to the earth in space ships, and to have departed the same way. It is claimed that the present cavern dwellers, and their counterparts on other planets, still use the space ships. If space ships are illogical, then the entire contention falls. Doctor (3), that is one of your pet subjects. Are space ships, and life on other planets, scientific possibilities?

(3) Emphatically yes! If some of the boys from the guided missile project were here, they would make it even more emphatic. We ourselves are right on the threshold of space travel. It needs only a very little more data, which could be secured by more or less routine experimentation. It is quite possible that some other beings are more advanced than we, and have already solved the problems.

How soon we humans will make our first voyage into space is mainly a matter of funds. Space craft, even small ones carrying only instruments, would be expensive to build. We might have to build several. It is almost impossible to foresee every problem which will be encountered. Our first craft might be failures, from the layman's point of view, but, from these failures, we would gain the information which we needed to succeed. This would all take money; large amounts of it. So far, no government or group has been sufficiently interested to advance the funds. Meanwhile, the army, and a private group headed by Willie Ley, continue their experiments, but are badly hampered by lack of funds, and their progress is consequently slow.

If the funds should become available, I have not the slightest doubt as to our ability to successfully construct space ships. I recognize no limitation this side of the infinite on the possibilities of science. What men can imagine, man can accomplish. The only reason we cannot accomplish beyond the infinite is that our minds, in their present state of development, cannot imagine beyond it.

As for the possibility of intelligent life on other planets, I can see no other logical conclusion. There are, in our own solar system, two other planets which, so far as we can deduce from this distance, are possibly capable of supporting life forms similar to our own. The life forms with which we are familiar are based upon the carbon atom, and depend, among other things, upon the principle of oxidization, which dictates certain limitations of temperature and atmosphere. The carbon atom is not the only possible basis of life. The similarity between the carbon and silicon atoms immediately suggests the possibility of silicon based life forms, which would probably have entirely different temperatures and atmospheric requirements.

Besides our own solar system, there are millions of stars, most of which are believed to be solar systems similar to our own. It would be conceited to the point of insanity to assume that, of these countless planets, ours is the only one capable of supporting intelligent life.

(5) Are you familiar, Doctor, with Mr. Shaver's theory of acceleration in space?

(3) Mr. Shaver may have been the first to publicly comment upon this, but I have heard it discussed by others long ago. It is merely an extension of the orthodox mass-acceleration formulae. Briefly it is this:

MASS is a relative and variable factor. Here on earth any object, a space ship, for example, would have a certain mass relative to the earth. As it traveled away from the earth, its mass would decrease, roughly as the square of the distance. At the same time, it would be under the mass-influence of all the other bodies in space, in the same ratio. At some points in space, these forces would be in an approximate equilibrium. At such points, the mass would be zero. If there is no mass, there can be no inertia, because inertia is dependent upon mass. If there is no inertia, then an infinitesimal force will produce an infinite velocity.

(M) At this point, Doctor, some of your students will ask: if you have no mass, how will you produce your force?

(3) By the expenditure of energy in the form of a rocket blast, to mention only one method. Any action must produce an equivalent reaction. That, so far as we know now, would hold true regardless of mass. I'd like to make it so clear that I am not claiming that the conclusions which I have cited are true. We won't know that until we get out into space. According to our accepted formulae, they are true, but errors and paradoxes have been found before. It was once conclusively proven, by facts which were considered sound at that time, that an airplane could not fly—but it does fly!

I should also like to point out to the young gentlemen of my classes who may read this, that, from the philosophical point of view, there is no such thing as a fact. Every fact, every law, every theory, in every branch of science, is based upon an unproved assumption and is, therefore, possibly in error. That assumption may have an overwhelming weight of circumstantial evidence behind it but, in the strict sense, it has not been proven. What we do is to examine the sum total of our experience in any field of endeavor and, from that, deduce certain things which we thenceforth regard as facts. If our experience has been broad enough, our conclusions are likely to be correct. Otherwise, we may have to later revise our facts to agree with reality. Our experience in the fields of physics and mechanics have been very broad—on our own planet. The probability of our theories in these fields should be very high—on our own planet. Our experience with them in space is nil. Whether they would still hold true there, remains to be seen. That is one reason why we are so anxious to get instrument carrying ships out into space. I do not mean to say that we should disregard our present concepts lightly. The preponderance of experimental evidence behind them makes their probability high. But we should not permit ourselves to fall into a blind and slavish acceptance of them under any and all circumstances. Under conditions different than which are familiar to us, they could be wrong.

(M) During the recent flying disc scare, the discs were immediately connected with the cavern theory. I do not know that Mr. Shaver ever made such a claim, but many of his followers did. Doctor (3), while we are on the subject of space ships, what is your opinion on this?

(3) Why pick on the flying discs in particular? They are only the most recent of

a long series of similar reports. The Biblical stories of the prophets ascending to heaven on a pillar of fire could, if we felt so inclined, be considered as reports of space ships leaving the earth. People have been seeing mysterious objects in the sky ever since then.

Some of the reports can be eliminated at once, because the mental unsoundness of the observer is obvious from the report itself. Others are clearly reports of some natural object, such as a meteor, or a strange, but not unknown cloud formation. Others eventually prove to be mirages. I should like to explain, because of the popular misconception on the subject, that mirages are not hallucinations. They are true reflections in the sky of actual objects on the surface, often great distances away. They are due to certain atmospheric conditions, can be seen by anyone who is at the spot at that time, and can be photographed.

When all these cases have been eliminated, there still remain some to be explained. Either we do not have all the information needed to classify them, or there actually was some object there. Into the latter category apparently fall such cases as the objects seen in the mid-west in 1897, in New England in 1908 and 1909, and, last year, the flying discs. There were many reports about all these which were plainly hoaxes, or the rambling of disordered minds (as invariably happens when any mysterious event occurs), but there were many others from persons of unquestionable reliability. Certain details, which I will not review at ths time, seem to rule out any possibility of mirage or natural objects. The only remaining conclusion is that they were either unknown aircraft or space craft.

In the case of the flyng discs, our government and all foreign governments have denied ownership, or any knowledge, of them. There are very strong logical arguments which tend to confirm these denials. If they are not of extra-terrestrial origin, then they must be the work of some unknown group upon our own planet.

(M) We note that Mr. Shaver frequently alludes to myths and legends, particularly the old Greek legends, as supporting the facts of the Elder Race and the events which he mentions. Doctor (5), you are an archeologist and our expert on ancient history and literature. Can myths and legends prove any fact, or should they be dismissed as pure inventions by our primitive ancestors?

(5) Myths and legends cannot be dismissed as pure fabrications, as they are invariably based upon fact. They could be correctly defined, I believe, as obscure, and usually distorted, versions of actual events. To clarify my statement I shall have to digress from Mr. Shaver and touch upon the general subject of the formation of myths and legends.

The origin of most myths and legends is lost in antiquity. The cultural level of the human race at that time was very low. They had no written language, and little understanding of scientific facts which we consider elementary. Events which to us would be quite ordinary would, to our early ancestors, have appeared miraculous. His lack of understanding would make him a poor observer in the first place, and his report would further suffer from word of mouth transmission. As it passed from person to person, and generation to generation, it would be subject to the natural human tendency to magnify, distort, and embellish. This trait can be noted even today in the fantastic distortion of word of mouth rumors. By the time the myth or legend would be recorded in writing, it might bear little resemblance to the actual event. However, it would still be the report of some actual event, no matter how distorted it might be. Something, at some far distant time, did actually occur, and made a sufficiently vivid impression on the observer to be remembered. By taking into account the social and intellectual level of the people, we can deduce the manner in which they might distort it, and are often able to get a fairly good idea of the actual event itself.

The events which Mr. Shaver relates could quite rationally be the basis of the myths and legends to which he alludes. They are not the only basis. Other events could be cited with equal logic and reasonableness. Mr. Shaver claims to have secured his information from the actual historical records of this ancient race. There is a possibility that, instead he has taken the myths and worked them back to a fictitious origin. If so, I give him credit for very excellent powers of logic and deduction, because he has arrived at a very logical answer. It is worth noting that the folk-lore of all peoples contains some account of individuals, or groups, usually of gigantic size, who had such remarkable powers that the early peoples regarded them as gods. These tales are undoubtedly inaccurate in detail, but their very consistency would indicate that there was some superior race on the earth in early times.

THERE is also concrete evidence of some such superior race. For example, the length, width, and height of the Great Pyramid in Egypt are exact fractions of the equatorial and polar circumference, and equatorial diameter of the earth, respectively. The ratios are so exact that it is only in recent times that our means of measurement have been sufficiently precise to verify them. To assume that all three dimensions just happened that way would be stretching the probabilities of coincidence quite a ways. The natives of Egypt at that time were semi-barbaric. They were patently incapable of the science and precise workmanship which would have been required. Most Egyptologists now agree that the Pyramid was built, or at least designed and supervised, by some non-Egyptian race.

To cite another example: there is an ancient temple in South America built of huge stone block which interlock without mortar. The joints fit with such precision that we would have trouble duplicating it today, even with all our precision machine tools. The work was obvously beyond the abilities of the Indians who later occupied the temple. They themselves have legends of a gigantic super-race which built it, and then departed by means of great tunnels.

I shall not take the time to cite further examples, but there are enough others to firmly convince me that there was upon the earth in pre-historic times some highly advanced race. This makes Mr. Shaver's claim possible, but not, in itself, necessarily probable. It does not necessarily follow that this super-race was as he describes them, or that they still exist. Both of those points will have to be established by further evidence.

(M) I think that the plausibility of the caverns themselves would be next in logical order. How could such an extensive cavern system exist without having been found in some of our mining operations? How could the entrances be so well hidden that they would not have been accidentally discovered by this time? Doctor (3), will you comment?

(3) As nearly as I can gather, Mr. Shaver places these caverns and underground cities deep in the earth, several miles below the surface. From what we know of the radiations of nuclear fission, and his detrimental rays appear to be something of the same nature, such depths would be quite logical, since a considerable thickness of earth would be necessary to absorb them. These depths are far below our deepest mines and wells, and would not thus be discovered.

Such underground works would have to have connections to the surface for access and ventilation. From Mr. Shaver's stories I gather that, in very ancient times, each underground city had its surface counterpart which served as a trading post between the cavern and surface dwellers. When the Elder gods left the earth, many of these entrances are supposed to have been closed. As communications on the surface improved, discovery of the caverns became more likely, and many of the remaining ones were closed by the people who then inhabited the caverns. It is said that there are still entrances and ventilating shafts, but that they are in isolated spots, and occasionally barred by movable rock barriers. In some of the stories, these entrances are placed in natural caverns, or abandoned mine workings.

It seems to be Mr. Shaver's contention that these entrances are found by surface dwellers at times, but that few return to tell the tale. If they fall into the hands of the deros, they are likely to become the main attraction at some sadisic orgy. If they fall into the hands of certain other groups, they may become serfs. They occasionally return from the caverns, but these few find that their tales are not believed, and either soon learn to keep quiet about them, or else end up in a mental institution.

As for the caverns, they could exist. As for the manner in which they are said to have been constructed, this is outside any scientific knowledge which we have today. The subject of temperature is open to question. Our experience in deep mines has been that the temperature increases one degree in each sixty feet. If this rate of increase remains constant, the caverns would be very hot places indeed. On the contrary, Mr. Shaver describes them as being very cool, 53 degrees, as I recall. In fairness, I must point out that we are basing our idea of cavern temperature on the assumption that the rate of temperature increase remains constant, and this may not be correct. In our stratosphere, for example, it was found that the temperture fell as we went up, and it was assumed that the trend continued to the absolute zero of space. High flying rockets seem to indicate, however, that the trend reverses at certain points, and that there are also some very hot bands above us, while astronomers now believe that there are also some warm spots in space itself. Some similar conditions might exist in the downward direction.

(M) As you are probably aware, Doctor, the interest in the Shaver mystery has revived interest in a number of so-called mysterious caverns. I think a word from you about these would be very much in order.

(3) There are a great many caverns which are locally regarded as mysterious. Most of them have never been completely or competently explored, and we have little or no really accurate information about them. Some of them are apparently artificial. I think it is a good thing to explore them if it is done properly. However, I would very much hate to see the attempt made by persons, or groups, who were not qualified or prepared for this kind of work, as this might lead to some tragedies. Eliminating the possibility of meeting some of Mr. Shaver's deros, there are many natural hazards in cave exploration. The field study groups in geology classes are occasionally taken into caverns, but only into those which are considered safe, and even then all precautions are taken.

They should be capable of judging the safety of the roof of the cavern, should maintain a guard against gas, with canaries or waltzing mice, and should have adequate supplies and equipment. I cannot, in a few words, cover all the important points but, if they are not familiar with working underground, they should seek the advice of experienced miners or cave explorers before going into a strange cavern.

(M) Our next question is on the Shaver claim that, along with the beneficial rays from our sun, there are certain rays which cause aging and other ill effects and, that if these rays could be eliminated, the life span would be extended indefinitely. Doctor (4), will you comment?

(4) In working with the atomic bomb, it has been noted that premature aging is one of the symptoms of radiation poisoning caused by emanations from nuclear fission. These same radiations are present, in very small quantities, in natural sun light. Whether they are the sole cause, or even an important contributory factor, in natural aging is not known. Certain physicists and biologists believe that to be the case. To date, no method of neutralizing or counteracting radiation poisoning has been found, altho research on the problem is in progress. Some of these research workers believe that, when an effective treatment for radiation poisoning is perfected, it might be used to arrest, or even reverse, the natural aging process, thus extending the life span materially. In the present stage of development all that can be said is that several very competent scientists believe in something essentially the same as Mr. Shaver's claim, but that nothing has been definitely proven as yet.

(1) If I may introduce a philosophical note into the discussion, I would like to observe that one very eminent biologist of my acquaintance has refused to work on this particular project because he believes that the result would not be socially desirable. Beginning in infancy, and continuing thruout life, an individual acquires certain patterns of thought and action, better known as habits. These become more firmly fixed in their mind as time goes on. If the process were continued long enough, their entire mental and physical life would be rigidly governed by these patterns. The brain would resist any change, and the individual would, therefore, become detrimental to, and parasitic upon, society.

This danger is illustrated by Mr. Shaver's description of certain of his Elder cavern dwellers who, by artificial means, have prolonged their lives for incredible lengths of time. What he pictures is a mere blob of almost inert organic matter. It has not the slightest interest in any material thing which does not concern its own welfare, nor the slightest human emotion toward any other individual. This, I believe, is a very good picture of the logical and eventual outcome of indefinitely prolonging human life.

THE USUAL picture, as it appears to me in the stories, is a medieval organization consisting of one Elder god of incalculable age in each group, surrounded by, and parasitic on, a number of younger, and lesser followers. The social organization brings to mind that of a bee hive or ant hill, where the entire effort of the group is centered upon maintaining one queen. Only, in this case, the central figure serves no useful purpose, so far as I can see, which makes the entire set-up seem asinine.

(4) I am afraid, Doctor, that I must register an exception to the spirit of inevitability which seems to pervade the theses of yourself and your colleague. It is true that some, from sheer mental inertia, fall into fixed mental patterns which occasionally become so deeply embedded that psychiatrists find it virtually impossible to alter them. On the other hand, I personally know many persons of advanced age who are still mentally alert and fully receptive to any reasonabl new concept.

It is my contention that physical aging is, in itself, an important causitive of mental inertia. The realization that the physical powers are waning, and that the end of useful life is approaching, comes as a severe psychological shock to many persons. Many gynecologists believe that this one factor is the chief cause of the various psychopathical and pseudo-physical disorders of women during the menopause, and of similar conditions in men during the climatic period of their lives. The feeling is one of insecurity and great mental uncertainty. The reaction is to hold fast to what they have, in both the mental and material sense. The result is extreme conservatism. I firmly believe that, if the period of physical vigor and well-being could be indefinitely extended, much of the ultra-conservatism and mental stasis associated with old-age would disappear.

(1) It was not my intention to imply enevitability in the strict sense of the word. However, I still contend that there would be such a strong trend toward what I pictured that it would be virtually inevitable. An increase in the life span would probably also increase the length of useful mental activity, as Doctor (4) has pointed out, but I do not believe that the final result will be altered.

It must be kept in mind that we are not discussing the increasing of the life span by two, or three, or any number of times. The proposition is that of extending it *indefinitely*. Some may hold that this makes the discussion entirely hypothetical. I do not share that belief, and several eminent biologists do not share it. If I do not believe that the proposition was scientifically possible of attainment, not in our time, perhaps, but ultimately, I would not waste my time discussing it.

Perhaps, in my original statement, I did not make clear what I had in mind. There would come a point in our almost-immortal man's life when the very variety and breadth of his experiences would cause him to become surfeited with every human occupation and diversion. At this point, his mind would automatically seek a psychological escape from the ennui by turning inward upon itself; devising and contemplating pleasant and fanciful situations; "day dreaming" on a grandiose scale.

The brain would resent and resist any change which involved mental or physical effort, because this would take it out of its pleasant dream world. The thing that contained the brain; I hesitate to call it a man; would, therefore, oppose and resist any progress, or any other change in the familiar and established order of things. Thus it would become a menace to society, because the maintenance of the status quo is an impossibility. No matter how high a science has gone, it has never reached its ultimate potentiality. It always can be and must be, advanced further. It is an inescapable law that nothing can remain static. It must either advance and grow, or decay and die.

When this intermediate stage had passed, and the creature had sunk into its dream world, it would cease to be an active menace, but the organization which it had formed might continue the evil work. In any event, it would be serving no good purpose and would, therefore, be parasitic upon society; unless you believe (I do not) that some good in the field of theology or metophysics might ensue.

When this problem is solved, we shall not have discovered the secret of life, the Sunday supplement writers notwithstanding, because we shall not, as a necessary result, have the ability to create true life. I do not believe that we shall ever have that ability. A finite mind, by its very nature, is incapable of ever comprehending the infinite forces which are involved in the creation of life. All we shall have discovered is the means of prolonging life which has been created by a higher Intelligence. I do believe that we shall discover that. I do not know how soon. Whether some other being have already discovered it, as Mr. Shaver claims, I do not know. When it is discovered, I believe that it is likely to be a curse, rather than a blessing upon mankind.

(M) If we have finished with that subject, we will go to the next. What is your opinion of the alleged ray mech, Doctor (3).

(3) All of the rays described by Mr. Shaver are beyond our science at present. Radar will bring us images of distant objects, but not in detail and not thru solid material. We know of certain rays which are lethal at distances of a few feet, but these particular rays, by their very nature, cannot be transmitted greater distances. We have

no ray which will blast or disintegrate objects.

Electrical transference of thought, or telepathy, has been the subject of experiment ever since the discovery of electricity, but we have not succeeded to date. We do know that the brain produces an electrical wave, and we have been able to record it and analyze it in a rather crude way. If this is ever perfected to the point where highly detailed variations can be recorded, then it might be possible to reverse the process and implant the thought in another mind.

MOST of the rays described by Mr. Shaver involve the transmission of considerable energy. This, our scientists cannot do, except on a very limited scale. A radio station transmits energy, but on a very small scale. Radar will set off photo-flash bulbs at a considerable distance, but here again the amount of energy transmitted is actually small.

To sum up, I would not care to call the ray mech impossible. Too many "impossibilities" have been accomplished to permit that attitude. They are so far beyond our present science, however, that I shall remain rather skeptical about them until more evidence is available.

(4) I do not think that skeptical is the proper word to use. As I understand its meaning, it impugns the possibilty of the proposition, and with that I cannot agree. Mr. Shaver's ray mech may be the invention of his own mind, or they may be real. That I do not know. In either case, I do not believe that he has described anything which is scientifically impossible. Let us merely say that our science has not yet advanced to the point where it can duplicate these rays.

Take his telaug ray for example, I can see one way in which it might possibly be done, because I have been toying, mentally, for several years with a very similar idea which I thought could be used as an electronic telescope, and which would work thru certain kinds of solid material. I was basing my hypothesis on the familiar radio principle of heterodyning, where two frequencies, brought together, will produce a third frequency which is the common divisor of the other two. What I had envisioned was transmitting two beamed frequencies, which could be a penetrating wave length, and bringing them to a focus at some distant point. The heterodyned frequency, which could also be of a penetrating nature, would be reflected from the distant object back to the transmitter. There, by means of further heterodyning, it could be converted to a visible frequency, and the distant scene reproduced on a screen. I have never had time to do any actual experimental work on this, and do not know when I ever will have the time, if ever. I am firmly convinced that something along that line could be worked out, however.

The principle would not have to be necessarily confined to the visual range. For example, Doctor (3) has noted that certain lethal rays are known, but that they can only be transmitted a few feet. It might not be necessary to transmit them at all. It might be possible to produce them right inside the vicim's body, by combining two frequencies which could be transmitted easily. If the principle works out, it has many angles.

Take another of Mr. Shaver's rays, his "stim ray". We already have the beginnings of that. I recently attended a demonstration of ultrasonics, that is: sound waves above the audible range. It is still in its infancy, but some of the effects stagger the imagination. It does have a very definite effect on the emotions at certain frequencies. At one point, everyone present had an overwhelming feeling of dread—of some impending doom. Another frequency went to the other end of the emotional scale and produced a feeling of light hearted gayety.

Coming to his thought tapes and telepathic mech, we also have the beginnings of something along that line. Besides the brain wave patterns which Doctor (3) mentions, let us consider the E.S.P. experiments which Rhine has been conducting at Duke University. This has been going on for several years now, and the weight of evidence is so heavy that it is no longer logically possible to deny that extra sensory perception does exist, and that it is possible to transmit thought from one mind to another. The means of transmittal have not been discovered, but it must necessarily be an energy wave of some variety. ·If the nature of this wave can be discovered, then it should be possible to record it, to electrically transmit it, and to synthetically produce it.

With regard to the transmission of power without wires; many years ago Nikoli Tesla worked out formulae and design details of a means of transmitting power without wires. Tesla's output of theory was prodigious, and he seldom bothered to verify them by experiment. Unfortunately, he had an enormous superiority complex, which he did not bother to conceal, and his published disclosures were usually filled with studied insult to all other scientists. As a result, he was thoroughly hated by all other scientists, and his claims were always greeted with sneers. Whenever he would condescend to demonstrate his own claim, or could goad some other scientists into trying it in an effort to prove him wrong, his critics were usually forced to grudgingly admit that he was right. The A.C. motor is a case in point. Our present motors, which really form the backbone of our industrial system, are, in every important respect, the same as the one which Tesla theorized and sketched up without experimentation.

In the case of his wireless power theory, he was building a transmitting plant on Long Island when World War I began. In the spy scare which followed, everyone with a foreign sounding name was suspect. Some bright boy in Washington got the sudden idea that Tesla's towers might be used to send spy messages to Germany, and ordered them to be destroyed. After the war Tesla declared that he had neither the time nor the money to rebuild, and was no longer interested in giving his invention to a people who were so incredibly dumb as to destroy it. The distaste for Tesla the man still obscures the brilliance of Tesla the scientists, and the experiment has never been made. There is some reason to believe that all the details were not revealed, and some further research work might be necessary. It is possible that the theory would not hold up if tried but, until we have tried it we cannot say that it is impossible to transmit power without wires. Just as an accused man is legally considered innocent until proven guilty, so the claim of a scientists of proven ability must be considered correct until proven incorrect.

To recapitulate; our science has not as yet advanced to the point where it can duplicate the mech described by Shaver, but there is nothing seriously improbable about them, and it is entirely possible that they exist.

(M) We have one other point before we close. Doctor (1) will you comment on the plausibility of Mr. Shaver's dero?

(1) Insanity of the particular form described by Mr. Shaver is quite well known, but such persons are usually put under restraint before they reach the acute stage of the deros. The condition could be caused by a brain injury, and such an injury could conceivably be caused by certain radiations. It is quite probable that environment would play an even greater part in creating such a group than heredity. According to the stories the ancestors of the deros seem to have been the lowest of the Elders, somewhat sub-normal, in the beginning. Close inbreeding, which would seem to naturally follow the conditions which are described, would intensify the defects, and tend to produce a moronic group. Children, growing up in an environment of evil, depravity, and sadism, would know no better emotions, and would probably never develop their nobler instincts.

To sum up; Such groups could logically exist, if the other condition were as Mr. Shaver describes them, and the dero is, therefore, plausible. It should be remembered, however, that there is a difference between plausibility and probability. All we can say is that Mr. Shaver, in describing his deros, has not introduced any impossible factor.

The foregoing is an actual transcript of a roundtable discussion held at a prominent Mid-Western University, the name of the school must be withheld for obvious reasons... As an interesting sidelight to this discussion, club members may not be surprised to know that the death of Nikoli Tesla, mentioned in the transcript, was predicted three days before it occurred by Richard Shaver. This can be checked through the editors of Amazing Stories............................Chester S. Geier

THE TERRIBLE CLOCK

BY RICHARD S. SHAVER

A WARNING TO ALL MANKIND

THERE is a clock of slow doom ticking, ticking. It has been doing so since Adam —since that Golden age that preceded the Adam legend—and for purposes of simplicity we will allow that Adam was the first to suffer from the effects of the ticking clock.

That clock today has come to be called the Geiger counter. But even though it had no name, the tick of its deadly message has been growing steadily in frequency since . . . Adam.

Time and radioactivity, so far as life are concerned, are much the same thing. One grows old because of radioactivity. One calls the process time, because one does not know any better.

But to those who do know better, the gloomy increasing tick-tock which has gradually cut man down from gigantic size to his present stature, which has cut his life span from the biblical Methuselah's to its present three score and ten—which has cut his mental stature quite as disastrously down from intelligence to the squamous morass of error we call thought today—in a terrible clock hanging on the wall of their minds, ringing out the inevitable doom of all man's aspirations. Just as surely as the crawl of the glacier, as the cooling of the sun—just that surely the radioactivity of the surface of earth increases—and has so increased since long before the deluge which gave the last death blow to the culture called the Golden Age—which is not even believed to have been anything but a legend by our present day "savants."

What man will become if he does not escape from earth and its doom is not pleasant to think about. Our life span is already so short that we just begin to learn what life is and what we should be doing with it—when we are too old to care what anyone does with it.

We are so little knowing about our earth and our life upon it that we do not even know that the life span is decreasing, or that the tick tock of the deadly clock goes on and on—more and more rapidly. We do not know that tomorrow's children will be less capable than yesterday's. Less virile, less balanced, less courageous . . . Pity man's children!

We have an illusion of prosperity and well-being and progress fostered by an "optimistic or bust" school of thought. Even our wars and mass murders, our steadily mounting catastrophes, plagues, murders, child delinquency—the list is endless—does not dispel this illusion of progress from the general mind. We spend our time placidly accepting the truth of a wonderful tomorrow for our children, and doing nothing about our worst enemies.

Those enemies are terrible, numerous, and powerful. Some of them are natural, such as the increasing radioactivity which is so little regarded or thought about. Some of them are alien humans, who spread wheat diseases to cut our food supplies, sabotage our commerce, spread disease for our people—and rob and murder without ever having the finger pointed at them directly.

None of these troubles are recognized by our press or our literature as anything but "natural," accidental obstacles to progress.

They are not accidental. They are purposeful, directed by intelligence of an evil, brutal kind. The race of man on earth, surface man—is today the most brutally mistreated people in history. And the most blind to their enemies.

The disc ships of their alien invaders are regarded by their so-penetrating press as "spots on people's eyes."

The A-bomb is regarded as the danger it is—and it is pretty evident they are *not* going to be able to keep it from destroying them.

The underworld, which has contained enemies for so many centuries, is still regarded as a fiction, just as always. The evil they do us is explained away by our learned ignoramuses as anything from "poltergeists" to "mass hypnosis" to "mob hysteria".

The good old U. S. A. is on the brink of its most desperate disasters of famine and failure of every productive faculty . . . and we call it a mild "inflation."

IT is time we get together and took a serious and sane view of our life and its terrible plaguing diseases, and started some counter-action against our destroyers.

Else "pity men's children" will be the laughing mocking catchword of the ZERVS who are taking over the surface of earth—they think—just as soon as we are sufficiently weakened.

"Zervs" you ask? "What are they?"

Zervs are just *one* group of those who are sabotaging our modern civilization, to replace it with a cruel, polygamous, barbaric dictatorship of their own—a society in which no scientist would work without a soldier at his back to insure his loyalty to the regime. In which no school child would read any book that did not exalt the dictator . . . "just like Hitler" you say.

It will be far different from Hitler's dictatorship. For *they* have the telaug, and no thought could take place without the ruler's spies knowing it. Every thought would be censored in the very brain it took place in. If the hostile thought persisted, the brain itself would be reduced to imbecility.

"Impossible," you cry?

No, little blind man, it is not impossible. It is taking place even now all around you. Many of your own thoughts are already the result of their implantation in your mind by the telaug.

Luckily many of these are your noblest thoughts, because we have still with us a good force of ray people trying to stem the growing tide of evil domination sweeping over the earth.

BUT they are failing, and you must be warned of their failure.

You must learn to fight your unseen, "incredible" enemies, quickly and well, you must learn that. Else you will be lost in a terrible system of life in which no tiniest *thought* can exist in freedom.

"If that is true, what are we to do?" you ask. Then you add, so easily, so confidently, "But it is not true, it is a hoax, it is Shaver dreaming up phantasms to entertain us."

But it *is* true, and I don't know what to do either. That is up to your leaders, your courageous, thumpingly-ignorant little elected Napoleons. I can only tell you and *hope* something comes of my already-late warning.

But you *know!* As you look about at your society and see the simple ills these leaders are unable to combat effectively, you know they are inadequate to face any such bug-a-boo as I depict.

So I counsel that you among you who can understand, try to do something a little different than to wait until you too need food and shelter as the people of Europe need them, today.

Do you think there will be a great "foolish" big-hearted America to send them to you?

You will starve and die without any such relief system.

Make an effort at least to understand *what* is happening to you. It is not all, all "accidental misfortune." There is a well organized "pattern of destruction" inflicted upon the U. S. A. and it is not even recognized publicly. You *should* know; you little good-hearted incredulous dupes.

For you are *not* little, but potentially the greatest people on earth. And you are losing that greatness to an unseen enemy; a cruel, brutal and utterly secretive enemy who "does not exist" too, too thoroughly.

You rich of the U. S. A. who feel so safe—are you safe? You know better, but what are you doing about it? Are you *trying* or *accepting* the system that is destroying you root and branch. That is making your children stupid and deformed with unseen rays over your estates one by one . . . or are you all already the victims of the "unseen" predators? Are those mansions of which even the common man of the United States was so proud already inhabited by the alien predator—pretending to be the same old family who built America up from a wilderness—the same ones who developed the reaper, the machine tool, the motor,—the threshing machine, the motor car— the electric power systems?

Or are they filled with masqueraders preteding to be our own rich? Who can say?

SCARY, wild things to say; hard to believe? Insane to think our country is falling to an alien; unknown publicly. Foolish to think there is a class of people who enjoy infinitely greater fullness of life to that which we call living, and who secretly vaunt and mock us—while they continue to despoil us of every last fibre of the value in our society, who prey upon us greedily, insatiably, and will so prey until as a people we have perished!

Those people who are *not* our rich, those enemies! They are *not* from among us, *of the soil* of the U. S. A. And they have power, and are evil—so far as we are concerned!

Pity the children of the world, when *they* at last hold all of earth under their brutal hands. Men will become less than medieval serfs. Man will support a terrible and haughty corruption which will leave him far less than crumbs. It will leave him only death, a death of all that he hoped to be—a death-in-life far worse than the serf's historical plight.

Which is of course all the raving of an alarmist. There is really no hidden danger, ever. This, too, is a phantasm for a fool's imagination. There is no sense to these words of mine. I write them only to amuse myself and befool you, the noble inheritors of all the good things of earth and life. No one else wants these things, there are no people planning to destroy you. And that is the truth, these are the ravings of a man wro does not know what he is talking about. There is no weapon in existenece which can destroy a mind from a distance. There is no telaug in existence. There are no secret destroyers of men's progress. There is no group who want the common man much *lower* than he is—and there are no rich who are jealous of our own rich, angry at their way of dispensing justice and freedom and upholding the Constitution which has made their country healthy and given them the fertile field in which their wealth could grow.

There are no cruel and brutal aristos left on earth, and monarchies are out of style. The era of freedom is ahead—not behind. There is no danger, Germany has fallen.

But the power behind Germany has not fallen!

The cult of the superman goes on!

Give it what name or form you want, the motives and the actual groups who caused all our troubles the last four decades are still alive and planning.

They remain, as always, behind the scenes . . .

And the terrible clock of doom ticks on and on, more and more rapidly. The deadly growing force causes steady deterioration of the fibre of man's character . . . or does it? Does "de" exist?

It is so very easy to be optimistic. It takes courage to face trouble and recognize how terrible is the future that we take no measures to alleviate.

Much could be done against increasing radioactivity. It is a problem not even attacked! Energies might be developed which could cause radioactive matter to decrease in radioactivity.

But being optimistic and incredulous of all danger will not accomplish it.

Our secret enemies could be exposed, resistance to them organized. But it will not be done by refusing to admit their existence.

You will continue to be optimistic about your future, mankind . . . until it too "does not exist!"

Pity men's children! The terrible clock ticks on . . . and on.

READER'S SECTION
Continued from page 5

truth. That is the whole purpose of the Club.

I have read both issues of the magazine with great interest, and will give you my honest opinions of "Mandark" when I have finished reading it all. In the meantime, congratulations to you for doing a grand job with all this, and best wishes for the future. . . . Howard B. Mac Donald, 171 Ravine Ave., Yonkers, N. Y.

Dear Mr. MacDonald:

If you looked up my record you would find not one, but three escapes. I went back and served out my time to clear it all up. You would find a lot of things I don't mention, too, so maybe you better just take my word for it. I mean well. I doubt if the police would just hand out my dossier to anyone, but they might. I never asked them. Leave them alone, as long as they're satisfied so am I, is my policy. Ding 'em.

I don't believe the police would consider my unexplained absence as any proof of anything except that give a dog a bad name, he'll have the game, or something like that.

The Shaver Mystery can't fall flat when people report flying saucers, can it?

Eventually we will prove it without proving me a felon onconverted, I hope.

Thanks for your congratulations, and let me tell you you haven't seen anything yet. . Shaver.

Dear Mr. Shaver :

Perhaps you have heard of the Mystery Spot before this, but in the event you haven't I'd like to relate one of the most eerie sensations it has been my good fortune to experience.

I don't happen to be one of those people that experience voices in the dark, visions, burning feet, poltergeist phenomena nor any of the other "out of the norm" occurences that the Shaver Mystery Club is dedicated to unveil, investigate or expose, although I must admit a more than usual curiosity regarding same even to the extent of buying both Charles Fort's book and Oahspe.

To get at this Mystery Spot. It is 3 miles out of Santa Cruz, California in a rather rough and wild section. The best explanation of it is, to me at least, the same action a "force ray" would give.

Explanations, scientifically have been given as "a negatively charged meteorite that has been buried in the hill, "an escape of gravity" unexplainable and so forth.

To cite some of my experiences while there.

Upon alighting from the car, a noticed slight dizziness—such as one experiences after a few quick shots. A tightening around the skull that became more pronounced as we came closer to the main region of inuence. Yet, it is commercialized.

Upon paying our fee we were shown the demonstration of the strange height differentiator which consisted of two concrete blocks exactly on a level (with a carpenter's level to prove it.)

A person standing on each of these blocks amazingly changed height when positions were interchanged. I can vouch for this because I was one of the parties, and although the man with whom my exact height when on the ground, when standing on one of the blocks I seemed taller, and when on the other block I seemed smaller.

My young son went through the demonstration with a boy taller than he, and when he got on the 'higher stone" he was the same height. When he stepped down to the other, there was a distinct appearance of stepping into a 3 inch hole.

The climb up to the main center of repulsion was an arduous climb of thirty feet or so at an elevation of 300 feet, but it seemed 10,000 feet. Later it was explained to us that the shortness of breath and the energy expended to make that short climb was caused by the resistance of the "repulsion force."

After arriving at the main center of force it was easily believed. It was possible in fact imperative, that one lean into the force at about an angle of 50 degrees to maintain ones balance. Farther toward the center it was exhausting to face the flow force. The slightest losing of balance would throw you farther away just as though a 40 or 50 mile gale were blowing.

Another demonstration of height differentiation was given—in which I demonstrated—only this time there was almost a foot difference.

There was no satisfactory explanation of the phenomena given because none is known I'm sure.

I repeat—in line with your reasoning—a force ray left untended and deserted could cause such an experience of repulsion. Take it for what it is worth, I can give no other explanation, perhaps you or others could.

To say the thing is really something and not faked is for sure. . . . Carl C. Berglund, 1630 Brookside Drive, San Pablo, Calif.

Dear Mr. Berglund:

I've heard of this Mystery Spot before. With your data to go on, I should say the phenomenon is due to an untended or deserted ray mech. In cavern warfare it frequently happens that the operators of a ray mech are killed leaving the ray still in function. And this warfar—as I well know—goes on all the time. . . . Shaver.

Dear Mr. Shaver:

As Popeye says "I yam what I yam". Now! How'd I get this way? Heredity, glands, diet, degree of evolution, environment, mental attitude, condition of soul, spooks, and now! rays.

Of course, wisdom to one is foolishness to another. But to me the "Shaver Mystery" dovetails myths, legends, religion, superstition, hel and the "boogeyman" into the only logical whole I know of. The Alphabet alone is amazing.

My experiences and the wide interest aroused seem to indicate there is a great possibility you aren't talking through your hat.

Can we organize and contact Nydia and her people and like groups? Get their cooperation and protection? Have them read surface minds and determine the trustworthy and efficient?

We will need plenty of backing. Not knowing who or what will oppose us. The degenerate dero ignorant, unorganized with only a hint of uses of the abandoned "mech" are formidable. If this planet is a wild life preserve furnishing zoo specimens or slaves for extraterestrials we can expect highly organized intelligence. If we are mere pets what whim or mood would we catch them in when attempting to better our lot? If an experiment, anything could happen. If occasionally raided by space pirates. If key figures on the surface are in cahoots, etc. on and on.

It may not be as hopeless as first glance seems. While it is no job for the timid or squeamish, enthusiastic, determined minds cooperating fully can do much.

Man is gregarious and the average knows cooperation is common sense, so, it must be "tamper" causing the silly desire to subordinate, exploit, and abuse.

As a machine gunner in one way I lost patience with that system of settling things. But if anyone or anything is carelessly, ignorantly, playfully, or through pure cussedness swishing rays around causing all the selfishness, clanishness, intolerance, bigotry, and two timing let's get busy.

Another angle, or danger, many surface people are slaves to their desires if they had access to the "stim mech" it would mean more tons of dreaming useless flesh added to that in the caverns.

It would be nice if we could board a spacecraft and wave to "Old Sol" saying, "It's been ageing knowing you", as we headed for a land of perpetual youth. If we can't do this ourselves, there is real enjoyment in unselfish work, for future ones. Let's not take it laying down.

Don't know if this me can hold together and carry on after meeting the white whiskered gent with the scythe or not. If not, it seems a waste of something. After all the trial and error, blind alleys followed from one disillusion to another and the little knowledge gained a little of the lesson learned. Oh well, if so, the Buddhist Nirvani of pure nothingness isn't too bad.

I am encumbered and will whole heartedly, cheerfully dedicate the remaining years of my alloted three score and ten and all I am able to borrow. . . . C. M. Nix, Route 3, Dublin, Georgia.

C. M. Nix:

You sure have the right slant on what I have been trying to say. It is good to be so well understood. I too try to work for the future knowing there isn't much hope for us in our time.

You are wrong about stim. It would not make more tons of useless flesh. It would enrich life immensely, has vastly more important uses than just pleasure. Stim makes any organ more active, including the mind. It is a medical ray; the sexual use, to the Elder race, was incidental. It develops pleasure in other pursuits to the point where sex is secondary as a value. Its greatest value lies in making the brain vastly more versatile and able. Love is enobled because the mind is able to see and appreciate the more subtle and fragile thoughts aroused by love, the part of life we now blindly miss. The gross is seen as gross, rather than wallowed in. Stim is an evil only in evil hands.

Yes, we could organize and contact such people as Nydia. It would take about as much money as Frank Buck spends to outfit a movie company with wild life in an expedition. We don't have it. National Geographic has that kind of money. They spend it on Maya temple expeditions, not knowing what lies under the Yucatan mountains where the Mayas once flourished.

We have their co-operation and protection, but we can't get back and forth because entrances are few and far off. They manage what is possible with rays. A lot more could be done if we did so organize. This magazine is an attempt toward that end.

Dero tamper is one of the main sources of our mass conflicts. It only takes a few trivial "incidents" to plunge nations into war. Remember the first world wars beginning, a bomb, a carriage, a death? . . . Shaver.

Dear Mr. Shaver:

I should like to make a suggestion. Inasmuch as all the members of the club are interested in solving the Shaver Mystery I think they would be more than willing to form an investigation committee.

The committee would investigate whenever possible all the mysterious happenings and places sent in by the readers. Or at least the ones that seem to warrant an investigation. The committee would give a report of its findings in each issue and also photographs when they could be obtained.

The investigations could be financed by increasing the price of the magazine or by some other satisfactory method. I for one would agree to any reasonable method of getting substantial facts and I'm sure most of the other readers would feel the same way. . . . Leon E. Copeland, 303 N. Water Street, Peru, Indiana.

Dear Mr. Copeland:
This looks like a good idea, but it's up to the members of the club whether they wish such a committee formed and are willing to finance it. What do you say, members? . . . Shaver.

Dear Mr. Shaver:

L—la-ngai-ygg—Ia—Shub-Niggurath. Ph'nglui mglw 'nafh Cthulhu R'lyan wgah 'hagl fhtagn. End of quotes!

In other words, I have at last received my copy of the Shaver Mystery Magazine. I would at this point like to compliment you on the nice job you did on same and can appreciate the amount of work you must have spent in getting it together. No doubt your efforts will be unappreciated by some but I am sure there will be quite a few who appreciate your taking the time and energy for a doubtless troublesome and unrecompensed task.

Tis true, you are also expending considerable time and possible money in the venture but you are more or less defending yourself and your theories in effort to settle something once and for all. In any case, I believe the result will be worth the effort after things get going and the letters and items come rolling in.

I might mention Mr. Smith's cover was quite a cover—a few more like that and you will have all the boys rushing for the caves in droves—and wait for me!

My only objection was that it was too short but I realize that with the cost of printing etc., you did well to get out a nice a job as you did. I haven't had time yet to read much of it very carefully but it sure looks good. I have a quaint custom of not reading continued stories until they have been completed so it looks as though it might be a long, long time until I get to read MANDARK though from glancing through it, it appears it will be worth waiting for.

Had you thought of running an article on yourself? That is, where you came from, what sort of writing you had done before these things, if any, and what sort of guy you are—seems as though this sort of thing would interest a good many.

Wishing you continued success in your various ventures. . . . J. O. Cuthbert, Box 1736, Pittsburgh 30, Pa.

Dear J. O. Cuthbert:
Did you ever read Lovecrafts protege's story, The Mound? Better than Lovecraft, and it has some true data on the caves mingled with Lovecraft expansion. In a Lovecraft collection of storys.
Think mag will get bigger and cheaper soon. Got to get more subs, it's only paying expenses now. Printing costs are extreme. Notice the Chicago newspapers lately?
Better read Mandark now. It isn't so thoroughly integrated that the time element would confuse you. You don't read the bible at a sitting, do you?
I'm a painter, of a writing family. I don't get time to paint any more. I guess it was lousy painting. For work, I used to move trees, on wheels, not by hand. Now I write. I'm a spectator type. The guy with his hands in his pockets, who looks like somebody you know. Somebody is always walking up to me and saying—"You look just like a friend of mine." I answer 'em, now—with—"Well, I am a friend of yours, but we didn't meet before!" Rubber-face, thats me. Or rubber-stamp.
Thanks for your kind words. You look just like somebody I ought to know. . . . Shaver.

Dear Mr. Shaver:

I received my copy of our Magazine and I sure enjoyed it. A few odd things have happened since I received the magazine.

Driving home one afternoon I suddenly felt something very warm against my right leg. So warm I took my foot from the gas pedal and felt to see if sometehing was burning, but I found nothing. Two weeks later I felt the same sensation against my neck and right shoulder again—nothing. The first time was 5 miles from home and the second time was two miles from home. My last name has been called three times. Twice by a man in a loud voice and the third time by a woman whose voice seemed far away.

Just lately I was in a Barber shop and sitting next to me was a man reading a newspaper (The Daily News). When he came to the middle of the paper where the pictures are, I looked over his arm and saw a picture of a four engine plane with the tip of a wing broken and its landing gear crushed. A plan had crashed a few days before and I wanted to read the article. To my amazement there was no picture of a plane in the whole newspaper. Well, I told several people about it and I received some peculiar looks. But three days later a plane did come and hit the corner of a building on the field and he landed with a broken wing tip and busted landing gear.

I entered a local newspaper competition and the person who matched the most twins (there are 60 sets) wins the prize. A pair of hands were shown to me holding the numbers 56 (I wonder). The results of the competition will be published this Sunday August 24th.

Well things are sure getting interesting. An idea for the curing of Cancer has been put into my head. (That's the only way I can describe it.) But I guess you have read enough of this.

Would it be possible to have a meeting of the Shaver Fans in New York City some day and of course meet you and the Beautiful Blind Girl from the Caves, or it that too much to ask for. You must get this question very often. How can we help the people in the caves? ... Jack Douglas, 149-10 Brookville Blvd., Rosedale, N. Y.

Dear Jack Douglas:

So you know there is something to the Shaver Mystery because you have experienced some of the "phenomena" which our mentors insist are entirely imaginary.

Most people have, Jack, and refused the evidence of their own senses.

Sorry I can't let you meet the beautiful blind girl, I think she has been dead for several years. The deros that killed her are "hypostatizations of what men do not desire" according to my critics, whatever that means. I guess they mean they don't exist. I wish they didn't. ... Shaver.

Dear Mr. Shaver:

I have just now finished the Reader's Section of the Shaver Mystery Magazine. Thank you so much for printing my letter. Believe you me I was most thrilled to see it, as it is the first fan letter I have ever written.

However there is one mistake, whether on my part in the writing or on the printers, is hard for me to say, but my seeing the ship (?) occurred in 1934-35 not 1944-45. So much for that.

As I promised I'll add a little more. I'll start with caves.

I came from a small town in Southeastern Utah. At the head of the Grand Canyon of the Colorado River, to be exact. Now this town (Moab) is in a valley about 24 miles long and 3½ miles wide at its widest point. It sets down 1500 feet off the desert floor. One might almost call it a hole. The Colorado River runs through the lower or western end of the valley.

On a cliff overlooking the river, about 1300 feet high is a sort of cave. (Let me say here, that I have never seen this cave. Why? I don't know for sure, except I was never very interested when I was a child, though at times, my Dad and brothers have been there). Well this cave goes back in rocks for a short distance and then drops straight down for no one knows how far. The hole is round and the sides are smooth, as if having been bored with a monstrous drill. One can hear coming out of the depths, a roaring as of winds or rushing waters. There have been, from time to time, half hearted attempts to find out the depth, but so far only 3,000 feet have been plumbed. Ropes with lights have been dropped that far. If lanterns or candles were used the lights went out.

This is about all I know about the so called cave at present, but the next time I go home on a visit, I will go up there and make an exploration on my own, and take pictures.

This summer a man and his wife visited here from Oklahoma. He is a trucking contractor. He (I can't remember his name) a year or so ago was doing some trucking for the gas line being put in Tennessee. They were about 20 miles from Knoxville in the mountains. One afternoon his wife drove out from a small town where they were living to pick him up and take him home. She was about 3 miles from the job driving slowly when from out of the trees came a crowd of what she termed the most terrible looking people one can imagine. Most of them talked in a jargon she could not understand and she was scared for she was warned not to go into the mountains alone. But the most horrible of all was a man with only one eye in the center of the forehead, two women with three eyes, two in the normal position and the third in the forehead. And last but not least, was a man with legs like a frog. When he walked he hopped along in a frog-like manner.

She said they climbed all over the car pointing at her and jabbering. She said she was too frightened to yell for help. But luckily the men had quit work on the way home and rescued her. Needless to say she never went into the mountains again alone.

A number of times I have experienced what I term mental telepathy and then forgot about it. I have heard at odd moments for years someone calling my name. Always when I have been alone. Twice, when I have been walking on the street. With my husband, neither of us saying a word, I have heard a conversation between two men, going on in my head. This was before I heard of the Shaver Mystery. I remarked to my husband both times of the odd conversation running through my mind. So I thought maybe it was something I had heard at sometime or another and subconsciously just thought about it, so I didn't let it bother me. One night in 1944 (I don't remember the month) my husband and I were resting after work. It was a little after dusk, when we heard the sound of drums coming from a long way off. But—they were coming from under the bed. These drums were in perfect rhythm. We got up and moved to different places around the room, but nowhere could they be heard except around the bed. We puzzled about it for several days and even told the neighbors. Of course, they laughed at us and asked us where they could buy some of that stuff too. But we did hear them. The drums were heard in El Cerrito, California just one block from El Cerrito hill. Maybe others may have had the same or similar experience.

Now for the last and certainly most experience. In the Shaver Mystery Magazine I received yesterday there is a letter from a Gail Harvey of Racine, Wisconsin. In answer to

G.H. letter you advised her or him to try to get in touch with the ray people to help her mother. Well as I have had an ailment for several years I thought I'd experiment also. What could I lose? So, as you suggested, after I went to bed I began concentrating on the ray-people, mentally calling for them as I would if I were calling a station on the radio. I concentrated on this form for about 5 or 10 minutes. Then, believe this or not, there was a loud noise in my head as if I was in a quiet room and someone opened the door for a second into a noisy foundry. Someone or something shoted, "Hey, Cleo", or maybe it was "Ray, Cleo" and then the door closed. At the closing of the door (incidentally at the noise I jumped straight up in bed) I had the oddest feeling in my head for about 15 minutes and I could not even move my little finger. I don't know whether I can describe the feeling but I'll try. As I said the feeling lasted for about 15 minutes. It felt like a very soft finger slowly and gently moving around, probing, ever probing. Not hurting but I could feel it moving in my head. Could I have contacted the Ray? I thought it could be so, so I thought of everything the Drs. have told me what the trouble was. All the time I was thinking these thoughts the probing continued when I had gotten through thinking as much as I know. The sensation went away and I found I could move my body again. I got up and found my body soaking wet from persperation. Upon going back to sleep I slept the first good nights sleep I have had in weeks.

What do you think Mr. Shaver? Do you think that I could have hypnotized myself into believing this thing really happened? I would very much like to know your opinion. . . . Mrs. Cleo Helmann, Richardton, North Dakota.

Dear Mrs. Cleo Helmann:

No, I don't think you hypnotized yourself. You called a friend, he examined you to see if he could help you. He did help you. You state that very clearly, why doubt it because it was a little different than an ordinary doctor coming to see you? You know what happened. You asked for it, and you received it.

Your letter about the mis-shapen people was interesting to me. It corroborates my own observations of one of the reasons for their secrecy—they are very different from us due to hereditary ray effects upon genes. Over so many centuries, ignorant use of extremely delicate and powerful apparatus which affects whole body of course has caused variations in reproduction, as so much of it is used for sexual stimulation and rejuvenation effects.

Twenty miles from Knoxville will be pinpointed on our maps. Interesting location, very.

About your date of seeing space ship, they have been seen at intervals for over a century, on record. How about those who saw them and didn't get on record? Vastly more. They must visit here often. They are an important part of our life, none the less signficant because so generally discredited as untrue. The flying saucers are real. . . . Shaver.

Dear Mr. Shaver :

I wish to join your club as I firmly believe in the Shaver Mystery for reasons I'll explain in this letter. When I read "I Remember Lemuria" the story struck a familiar note in my mind as regards something that has been bothering me since my first memories.

I was born with a veil, and am very good at future predictions, when I want to concentrate or use thought waves. I'm a dancer by profession, and this because of what might be called instinct rather than training. You see, I'm self-taught from dreams alone, which are so weird and real that I hate to wake up at times. When I meet musicians of my kind, I can inspire them with thought waves, because the dances are out of this world. I've proved it many times. I believe a ray mech is used.

I only meet musicians like that every once in a while, and have found a band that I believe will become famous, as they feel as I do. We plan to tour Mexico, Panama, and South America. I'm doing radium specialties, so called, using flourescent products. I'm afraid of radium. I've never had a sun tan in my life, as I'm afraid of the sun and get pretty ill when under it—sort of dizzy and foggy. I believe it's true that it is only safe to live underground. I'd love to experiment, but can't stop work long enough.

By the way, I'd appreciate hearing from members of the club. I love to receive letters, and will answer any as soon as possible. . . . Honey Harlow, 910 Lincolnway, LaPorte, Ind.

Dear Miss Harlow:

You be darn careful of that paint, it can kill you. And radium can too, and it's a nasty death. The black light fluorescent may be safe on the skin, but do you KNOW it is? Have it tested, don't take anyone's word for it.

Did you ever think what "on the beam" means? Could it be a ray beam, stimulating, conductive of thought, augmentative of thought, connecting you with the musicians? That's what you thought, too! I had heard show people knew something of this ray mystery, hope you can pick up more about it for us.

Certain skins can't take sun is true. Especially the "Honey" colored type. Don't try to, it will only make you sick. Your skin lets in more ultra-violet, you don't need as much in consequence. You can get all you need from ordinary light.

I think the Club members would get a kick out of writing to Miss Harlow. . . . Shaver. P.S. You be careful about Southern countries. Byrne tells me it's near sure death to try to live there, contagion, etc. The bad spots are very bad. And with your skin in a hot country, you'd be in a susceptible state of weakness from the heat. You have to watch every drop of water you drink, every thing you eat, to avoid illness.

Dear Mr. Shaver:

I have read the magazines from cover to cover. They are simply wonderful. The story "Mandark" I read with great interest. Whether it is true or not, it is good reading. It was not too much of a shock to me to read that "Jehovah", was a hugh Black giant of a man, or God as I have read or heard somewhere before, that he was of the "Ethiopian" race, and that the rulers of Atlantis were black men, who held the white men as slaves, then when the white man became top dog he in turn enslaved the black race. Perhaps that has something to do with the so called race hatred. The whites hate the blacks for enslaving them thousands of years ago. In fact away back in the days of Atlantis. And the black hate the whites for the same thing in our own modern times, as it was in the days of Abraham Lincoln. "The blacks became free men and women."

Has H. R. Wickline read "The Lost Continent of Lemuria", sold by the Rosicrucian order or A.M.O.R.C. of San Jose, California? Correction please, the book is "Lemuria, the Lost Continent of the Pacific", by W. S. Cerve. On page 122 it gives a description of the dwellers of Mount Shasta, whom they call Lemurians. That this is a true description I can verify as I have personally seen one of these strange men in the year 1935 or 36. He visited Watertown and sat beside me, though he did not speak. He was seen by different people. The police tried to arrest him, as they thought he was a refugee from an insane asylum, because of his strange actions, but he demagnetized their auto so it would not start, until he was safely out of their reach. There was quite a commotion in Watertown, over him. Neighbors reported he was seen hanging around my home, peeking into my windows; while I was at work. The police came to my home and questioned me at the time, but I was as ignorant as they. A few years later I sent for the above mentioned book and you can imagine my surprise to read a word picture of my "Mysterious friend," as I have nicknamed him. What he wanted with me, I have never as yet found out.

I have also a "Rosicrucian Digest", which tells of the Rosicrucians, helping these strange people to move, from Mount Shasta, as they were being annoyed by cave explorers, and many of them were killed by bombs being dropped into crevices in a useless effort to open an entrance into the caves. Though there are caves man can enter into Mount Shasta, the entrances to the Lemurian caves are so well disguised man cannot find them. I think these are the Secret caves a certain seer told me about, a few yars ago. That I will be taken into them by a giant of a man, through what would seem like solid rock to people who might be watching us. They will never be able to find the opening even though they almost blow the top off of it.

This seer told me many things that have happened to me, so this other thing may take place too. Much of it still is over my head. I have you to thank for certain things you have said, or written in your stories. They have been the key that helped me unlock a mystery that has puzzled me for years. He told me of a secret opening into an unknown cave right here under Watertown no one knows exists. That I am to find and will report to someone outside of Watertown and of a calling down I will get from the Watertown fathers or councilmen, for not letting them into the secret first. So far I have failed to find anything. I wonder if the cave in "Mass", mentioned in Ginger Zwick's letter is anywhere near Watertown. I would like to find out. . . . Kathleen Sullivan, 99 Arsenal Street, Watertown, Mass.

Dear Kathleen Sullivan:

There are many tales of "Atlantis." As I see it, they are legends of several surface races long vanished who had knowledge of the caves and hence had a modern type culture on the surface. Why did they vanish?

The scientists who hold that the deluge was caused by a moon descent, think "Atlantis" a legend of the times before the flood. That seems the most accurate account.

Glad to hear about your eye witness of a Lemurian. I didn't know the old accomplished race really still existed. Have several letters with similar accounts of seeing these people around Shasta. If they are of the old race it explains a lot. Wonder why they shun us so? Or is it obvious? Maybe it is.

Don't know for sure about near Watertown. My knowledge of Mass. ray leaves me shuddering. It's no place to go. There has been a lot of surface contact in Mass. There was a police attempt to stop ray deviltry there which failed. They built a big X-ray type weapon. When they tried to use it—they got killed. . . . Shaver.

Dear Mr. Shaver:

I believe that you should be able to enroll many members in the Shaver Club from the occupation personnel here in Japan. The supply of Amazing Stories is usually much in demand at the Tokyo PX counters. References to "Deros" are rather frequent in daily conversation.

I think Japan would be a good country to investigate regarding the Cave Dwellers. Japanese mythology contains numerous references to the cave people, and many Japanese in all levels of the population are more or less convinced that these people really exist. One new slant has been introduced here, however, and that is that the Japanese underground people frequently come to the surface to enjoy the cooler air and temporarily escape the oppressive and sultry atmosphere of the lower regions. As you probably know, Japan is of volcanic origin with many active volcanoes, so this does not sound too improbable. Furthermore, the Japanese Deros are not usually regarded as being unfriendly to the people. Most of the Deros are thought to be kindly disposed, with only a small minority actively opposed to the surface men, as well as to other Deros.

Their origin and historical background is explained in this way: ages ago, before the dawn of recorded history, the islands of Japan slowly emerged from the sea. This process was gradual and occurred over long centuries of time. The people of that day were accustomed to a heavy, "watery" sort of atmosphere, and as their world slowly entered the light of the sun, the people adjusted themselves to the new conditions, without trouble. A small minority, however, could not be comfortable in this new kind of environment, surrounded by an atmosphere which they called "firemist", so they banded together and sought caves of refuge where they could live in comfort. The present day surface men, presumable, are the descendants of those who proved more adaptable to the new conditions. It is said that the underground people possess many "magical" machines and instruments, but have lost the ability to use them effectively. These machines still exist, because they have been protected against deterioration by the favorable conditions found in the caves, and much of their equipment is still in a state of perfect preservation.

Occasionally, some adventurous Japanese claims to have been escorted underground to visit the friendly Deros, and to have been shown many of the curious devices in their possession, but this is not often believed by his friends when he returns. I am now endeavoring to get in touch with one of these persons, for I believe I could persuade him to show me where the cave entrance is located. One person in particular I am trying to contact claims to have visited the caves and been furnished with a complete set of maps showing the cave network in Japan, with a connecting tunnel, or tunnels, to America. It is reported that during the recent war, American and Japanese cave dwellers also took sides, made raids on each other's territory, captured prisoners, etc. Fortunately for all of us, they could not operate their tremendously powerful machines.

All of the foregoing is somewhat at variance with your account, but explanations of the Deros may be expected to vary in different countries, and I thought the Japanese version might be of interest to you. There is much more to say, of course, from the Japanese point of view, and if you wish further details I shall be glad to give you what information I can. . . . David Telford, Tokyo, Japan.

Dear David Telford:

I have contacted, in Mass., ray people who showed me a traveler of the caves from Japan, as well as two from Tibet. Your reports on general Japanese knowledge of these people are very interesting. Indians of America as well as So. Am. have a similar widespread knowledge and legend of the caves. You misuse the word dero. In the caves they really use the word "rod", and they are in the minority as you say, are not the cavern people, but their plague, as ours. The ancient word for good man was tero. This word is not used today except by Shaver fans. A dero is devilish to all good people. A tero is good people. You are a tero.

Interesting how the Japanese legends of the cave people and how they came to originate jibe with what I have heard. The caves run right on under the ocean, did you know the barbary apes cross under Gibraltar, show up on the rock from no one knows where? Rock at great depths is impervious to all water because compressed.

Your reports on Japanese and American ray raids are truth. I heard them too. I don't see the variance between your account and mine, and like you, I see it is lucky the Jap ray was not able to get the big mech in operation. There are few alive who know enough about it to operate the more complicated types of apparatus. These few are locked in combat with the devils who inhereit the knowledge from their forefathers, have little real thought. While these fight for possession, the caves are looted by aliens, as I get it, from space. The immensity of the caverns is one point hard to comprehend. They run under the seas and the land, tier on tier, making many times as much area as on the surface. . . . Shaver.

Dear Mr. Shaver:

I have just finished reading the first issue of The Shaver Mystery Magazine and part of the second. You explain things more fully than in Amazing for which I am grateful. The more I study this mystery, the more afraid I get, but I am still willing to help if ever the time comes.

Is the way you went into the caves now closed? If not why can't Nydia and others like her get some kind of concrete evidence to the surface people. If they really want our help they've got to come out in the open and prove their existence. But I guess if you could get such evidence you would have done so long ago.

Strange experience—I had a violent headache one day. Having nothing better to do, I started exploring it so to speak. "Why couldn't it feel good instead of bad?" "Why should it be a pain at all?" All the time I was trying to "see" the pain. Finally, all of a sudden I realized the pain was gone. Since then I have tried it many times. It doesn't always work and sometimes only partially. I can't do it with any other pain. My dreams were very vivid as a child. I could remember them after awakening. The only ones I can remember now that might have been "ray induced" are these. I was gazing at a huge building (pillared front). Sometimes I was outside and sometimes I could go in. It was very big and awe-inspiring. I always assumed it seemed so large because I was a child and that it wouldn't seem so big when I grew up. This has grown vague in my mind now and I can't remember any details. One more part of a dream I remember was a footprint in rock. I was a man and at first the print astonished me. Then, I remember, I realized I had made it myself. The sight of the footprint in rock is still very clear but the rest is forgotten.

I hope nothing happens to stop your work. If it does it would be only one more proof that there is something worth investigating. . . . Mrs. Grady Music, Box 614, Garberville, Calif.

Dear Mrs. Grady Music:

Why don't the cavern people like Nydia come out in the open? Because they are ridden by old custom, and by evil gangs who they can't circumvent, apparently. We are trying to help them accomplish that. But the entrances are either held by evil, or are in savage jungles remote from civilization. So we work as we are doing here. We do not expect much success, as even when things are out in the open, like the flying saucers, the officialdumb call them spots before your eyes. If it doesn't fall on your head, it ain't there.

You must remember that for the most part the cavern people are lost to man in an immensity of tier on tier of builded caverns, incomprehensible and terrible in their remoteness from contact with the surface. Between them and us is miles of solid rock, compressed by weight into an impervious thing which water cannot even seep through. The caverns are bone dry, dusty, the deeper ones hot. This barrier of super-dense rock is pierced by only a few openings over the whole surface of earth, and these openings are held by great strength because of the valuable trade. This battle around the entrances is the bottleneck. How can we remedy that? Such aliens as come here in the flying saucers hold some of the openings—or all? . . . Shaver.

FATE

The Magazine of the Strange, the Unusual, the Unknown

Is our planet being visited by ships from other worlds? Are there really sea serpents? Who was Baltazarini's Ghost? When will the A-bomb fall? Who were the Amazons? What science do the kahunas of Hawaii use in walking over hot lava praying enemies to death, reviving the dead, changing the future? Can man live and think without a brain?

FATE Magazine answers all these questions and many more!

Don't miss the Summer issue of the most unique magazine ever printed.

On Sale May 20 - 25c at your Newsstand

Or better still send in your subscription to -

FATE MAGAZINE

Clark Publishing Co. - 139 N. Clark St., Chicago 2, Ill.

$1.00 for 4 issues $3.00 for 12 issues